Nigel Tranter

Hope Endures

HODDER

A CIP catalogue record for this title is available from the British Library

ISBN 0 340 82359 3

Typeset in Sabon by Hewer Text UK Ltd, Edinburgh
Printed and bound by
Mackays of Chatham Ltd, Chatham, Kent

Hodder Headline's policy is to use papers that are natural, renewable and
recyclable products and made from wood grown in sustainable forests. The
logging and manufacturing processes are expected to conform to the
environmental regulations of the country of origin.

Hodder and Stoughton Ltd
A division of Hodder Headline
338 Euston Road
London NW1 3BH

Principal Characters
in order of appearance

Thomas Hope: Son of an Edinburgh merchant and French mother.

James the Sixth, King of Scots: Son of Mary, Queen of Scots.

Charles of Lorraine: French Duke of Mayenne.

Henry, Duke of Guise: Great French noble.

Harry Hope: Thomas's younger brother.

Sir Thomas Hamilton of Binning: Later Earl of Haddington (Tam o' the Coogate).

George Heriot: Goldsmith in Edinburgh, and banker.

Elizabeth Bennett: Daughter of John, laird of Wallyford.

James Stewart, Earl of Moray: Great Scots noble.

Ludovick, Duke of Lennox: Kinsman of King James. Lord High Admiral and Great Chamberlain of Scotland.

Patrick, Master of Gray: Said to be the handsomest man in Europe.

Queen Anne: Princess of Denmark. Wife of King James.

Thomas Howard, Duke of Norfolk: Earl Marshal of England.

Alexander Seaton, Earl of Dunfermline: Chancellor of Scotland.

King Christian the Fourth of Denmark: Brother of Queen Anne.

Sir William Alexander of Menstrie: King's Master of Requests, later Earl of Stirling, founder of Nova Scotia.

George Villiers, Duke of Buckingham: English royal favourite.

Prince Charles: Son of King James. Later Charles the First.

Princess Henrietta Maria of France: Later Queen of King Charles.

James Graham, Earl of Montrose: Later marquis and noted soldier.

General Alexander Leslie: Veteran Scottish soldier.

Oliver Cromwell: Great English Puritan soldier. Captain-General and Lord Protector.

Prince Rupert of the Rhine: Nephew of King Charles.

Archibald Campbell, Marquis of Argyll: Great Scots noble known as MacCailean Mor.

Charles the Second: Succeeded his father, Charles the First, as king.

John Maitland of Lethington, Second Earl of Lauderdale: Later duke.

General David Leslie: Nephew of General Alexander. Covenant leader.

Andrew Cant: Leading Covenant divine.

Lewis, Marquis of Huntly: The Gordon chief, known as the Gudeman o' the Bog.

William Keith, Earl Marischal: Hereditary leader of Scots army.

Sir Hector Maclean of Duart: Highland chief.

General George Monk: Parliamentarian English general. Later Duke of Albemarle.

I

Thomas Hope stared at his father. "You are . . . to die? Die! I knew that you were sickening. But to die! Must it be so? The physicians say it?"

"They can do no more for me, lad. But do not grieve overmuch. I have known that it would come to this for some time. They told me, the physicians. It comes to us all, one day. And I will go to join your mother again – Jaqueline. I look forward to that!"

"But when? When do you go, Father?"

"Soon, I am told. Sad I am, not at the dying, but that I will not see your graduation, when you, Thomas, become a writer, a lawyer. As you wish. In more than another year. That will be the great day. My son an advocate!"

"No. Not yet. Two years more, for that."

"Ah, yes. That for the advocate. But the lawyer sooner. Then you will earn your own moneys. You could do well, grow rich. Lawmen do well for themselves." He nodded. "But, meantime, you will not starve. My affairs are in good order, here in Edinburgh. And your mother's, in Dieppe, still better. You will fare well enough. And our house, in this Edinburgh here, Todd's Close, will serve you for your work when you have graduated, and still lodge you and your young brother, Harry, whom I must leave in your care, Thomas."

Henry Hope, burgess of the city, merchant-trader, patted the shoulder of the young man, scarcely more than a youth indeed at seventeen years. "To be left, at your age, to fend for yourself and your brother is hard. But you are of stout enough character, and will do none so ill."

Thomas shook his head, biting his lip. "To lose you. Left alone. With Harry. It is . . ."

"You have your uncles, my brothers Edward and Alexander and James. They will guide you, James in especial, since he is a lawyer, as you aim to be. And Edward is Guild-Brother, of note, and strong in the Kirk, even was friend to the man Knox – to whom he is welcome! As you know, I am less than fond of these reformers, as they call themselves. But their Kirk is becoming ever more powerful. So Edward could be of much use to you, perhaps."

"I mislike to have you talking to me in this fashion, Father," Thomas declared. "As though all was . . . over with you . . ."

"It almost is, lad. You must accept it. As I do. I have a great belief in the hereafter. So, sorry as I am to be leaving you meantime, I will be waiting for you, with your mother, in the other world beyond the stars. But meanwhile *you* have your mark to make in this life. I judge that you will do it to good effect. Make the most of college. And in time, as a lawyer, you could have great opportunities. This is a time of great change in our Scotland, the religious strife largely over, but much yet to be settled. The great Church lands are being divided up and fought over by the nobles, the new divines seeking to keep their parish bounds intact, King James requiring his share of it all, he a canny monarch, unlike his poor late mother."

"Two years yet, Father, ere I can act the lawyer. And who knows what will have transpired by then?"

"I will be watching you, from above. And, I judge, proud of my son. *Our* son, for Jaqueline will be with me again.

2

Sons, as Harry will no doubt make his own way. But guide you him, lad. At but fourteen years he needs some directing. I trust you to see to it, but three years older as you are, an early age for the like."

Thomas, tall, slender, already quite good-looking, nodded. "I will do what I can. And – this of Dieppe, Father? What would you have me to do there in this pass? I know that links there are of value. But . . ."

"Of major value, yes. Your mother, although from Paris, inherited much in Dieppe, in the province of Béthune – where the Beatons came from. Through her I became made a burgess of Dieppe, as well as of Edinburgh. It would be good if you could be so, also, for it is a rich, prosperous port and hinterland. Forbye, King James's mother, the late unhappy Mary, Queen of Scots, had Guise blood; *her* mother Queen Marie of Guise, sister of the Duke Henry and the Cardinal of Lorraine, had an inheritance in Béthune, which King James ever complains should be his now. I have sought to discover the truth of this, but so far have not succeeded. Perhaps, lad, if you could speak with the king, you might learn of it, to his advantage, and therefore yours. French law may be not so very different from Scots."

"Could *I* approach the king?"

"Oh, yes. James Stewart, whatever else, is approachable – aye, and likes other young men. So watch you, if you do see him! A strange man indeed, but clever."

"He will be at Stirling?"

"No doubt. He bides in that castle most of the time, preferring it to that of Edinburgh. Go see him, and tell him that you go to Dieppe. He may have tasks for you. To serve him there . . ."

So Thomas rode the thirty-five miles west to Stirling, where he viewed the great citadel on its rock-top, so similar to Edinburgh's, where James Stewart had been raised, and still looked upon as his home, its hereditary keeper his boyhood friend, the present Earl of Mar, as his father had been before him.

Thomas had no great difficulty in gaining admittance to the stronghold, young as he was, when he announced that he came to see King James on a matter concerning the Guise lands in France. He was told that His Grace was out hunting in the Flanders Moss, up-Forth, a favourite pastime. So he had to wait, admiring the prospects of the long line of Highland mountains to the north-west, and the Ochil summits to the north-east.

When the king eventually returned, flushed with his exertions and smelling strongly of a mixture of sweat and blood – not his own blood but that of the deer he and his party had managed to slay in the bogland of the Moss, for James believed that paddling his feet in the warm entrails of the deer was good for rheumatism – the odd monarch was in no state to discuss affairs in France with an unexpected young subject, even though he had heard of the Hopes, and said so. He was indeed an odd character, in looks as in all else, scarcely kingly. He was now aged twenty-five, of medium stature but gangly, slouching, knock-kneed, sallow of complexion and dribble-lipped, this because his tongue was too big for his mouth; a less likely son for the beautiful late Queen Mary would have been hard to imagine. And her husband, Darnley, had not been ill-favoured of feature. There were rumours that James's true father had been Mary's Italian secretary, David Rizzio; and the king's somewhat swarthy countenance did not contradict that.

"So – you're one o' thae Hopes, are you?" he greeted Thomas. "I ken Edward Hope, the Guild-Maister." James always spoke in braid Scots. "You'll be his laddie, eh?"

4

"No, Sire. He is my uncle. My father is Henry, a merchant-trader, of Edinburgh."

"Ooh, aye. And what want ye frae me, Hope man? Fowk aye want something, I've found."

"Only to speak of some matters that may concern Your Grace, of which I have a small interest. Touching on France, and your royal mother's links therewith. In especial with Béthune and Dieppe, where my mother hailed from, Jaqueline de Tott."

"Hech – Dieppe, eh? Béthune. Aye, yon's Guise country. A scoundrelly lot! I'm no' proud o' *them*!"

"My father is a burgess of Dieppe, Sire, as well as of Edinburgh. He trades there. How he met my mother. And he has learned that the present Duke Henry of Guise plans to sell the harbour-rights of Dieppe, which is the main port for Paris, a rich prize indeed, and to donate some of the proceeds to the Vatican, that prayers should be said for his immortal soul. But keeping most of them! Through his late uncle, the Cardinal of Lorraine, he has much influence in Rome."

"The Popish scoundrel! He'll no' can dae that! No' without the agreement o' others o' Guise blood, *mine* among them. My mother's share. He must be stopped. That is, unless he gies me an honest whack o' it. Thae harbour-dues will be worth plenties, aye, plenties. Ye ken the name Dieppe means just deep, the nearest deep-water port to the capital o' France, Paris."

"That is why my father sent me to see Your Grace. Your royal interests are involved, he says, as well as ours, or my late mother's. I was to learn how you see it, Sire."

"I see it as gey important, boy! But you are gey young, are you no'? To be seeing to the like. How old?"

"I will be eighteen years in two months, Sire."

"Just eighteen? Can the likes o' you deal wi' this?"

"I am trained in the law, Your Grace. I have not yet graduated, but I judge that I know enough to deal with this. I have studied French law also."

"Are you no' being ower brash? Judging that you ken it a', at your age?"

"I hope not, Sire. My father, he has told me much. He judges me able for this task."

"Ah, weel – you'll likely can dae nae harm to *my* interest yonder. And I ken nae ither like to be going there. So, dae your best, laddie, for mysel' also, and you'll no' suffer for it, I'll see to that!"

"Yes, Sire."

"Aye, and bring me back what you can learn o' it a', Hope man. I wish to ken."

Thomas bowed out.

So it was back to Edinburgh and Leith, to discover when a ship could take him to France, to Dieppe. There proved to be no difficulty in that, for there was much trade with that nation, and Dieppe its principal destination. He had only three days to wait.

His father gave him fullest instructions, and an introductory letter to the mayor of that city, of which he was a burgess, recommending that his son might be made a burgess also, despite his young age, in view of his knowledge of French as well as Scots law.

Three days later, then, father and son parted, the former declaring that he hoped still to be in this life on Thomas's return. But if not, he was sure, they would meet again, wife and mother with them.

The sail southward, in a vessel laden with wool and grain and whisky, took five days, calling in at Newcastle and

Hull to pick up more trade goods and a trio of merchants. From these Thomas learned quite a lot that might be of use to him. Where the River Arques reached the English Channel was the city of Dieppe, behind chalk cliffs. Quickly thereafter the river shallowed, so that large ships could not sail further inland, this accounting for the importance of Dieppe. It was a large commercial city, but dominated by a castle and cathedral, with innumerable warehouses flanking the lengthy dockland, shipbuilding yards, cloth mills and granaries. Thomas reckoned that there was fully a mile and a half of docks. The harbour-dues here would indeed command an enormous sum. His mother had been the daughter of a wealthy wool merchant here, who traded with Lammermuir sheep-rearers in Scotland.

Thomas's father had judged his task best started by introducing himself to the mayor of this Dieppe, and thereafter to the Guild-Master, using his sire's burgess-ship as commendation, and his mother's links with the city. He might also find some Tott relatives who could be helpful. His first effort, then, was to find the mayoral premises.

This was not difficult, large and busy a city as Dieppe was. The mayor, named Ferdinand Dieufoy, when he heard that here was a Tott kinsman and son of a burgess, was amiable, especially when the King of Scots' connection was mentioned, and James's opposition to Duke Henry's plans to sell off the harbour-dues. He and his magistrates and councillors objected strongly to these, indeed doubting whether the duke had the right to do so. Was it lawful? Thomas said that his father's view was that it was not, that the rights were vested with the citizens' representatives. He himself, although not a burgess, had studied French law, and believed that he could, if necessary, present that cause in a court of law. Mayor Ferdinand doubted his competence, so young a man; but when King James's authority was asserted, with the royal objections, he agreed that Thomas should see the city's legal representatives.

These, likewise, were sceptical over his youthful abilities; but this of representing the interests of the King of Scots was telling, and could just possibly give *them* the desired advantage against Duke Henry. But they were reluctant publicly to assert this, the Guises being so powerful. None of the legal fraternity was eager to appear in court pleading against that dominant family. Thomas offered, indeed all but demanded, to do so himself, in the name of his monarch; and this did impress them. They agreed to arrange a hearing before the province's justices, so long as it was this young Scot who did the pleading.

It was, naturally, a very real challenge for Thomas. But he believed that he had the right and the law on his side, and the city authorities were backing him, however discreetly and anxious not to offend the duke and his brothers, but were concerned for Dieppe's cause. If he failed, they could distance themselves from him, to be sure. Without King James's declared backing, of course, they would not have urged him to go ahead.

It took a little time, and much behind-closed-doors arranging, for the desired hearing to take place, in the city's justiciary court, Thomas meantime brushing up his French law most heedfully. Thanks to his upbringing by his French mother, he spoke that language almost as well as English.

It was a delicate situation, for and against. Thomas would have not only the citizenry of Dieppe but most of Béthune *for* him, however muted that support; and the so powerful Guises to oppose. And there was always the danger that the justices themselves would be prejudiced in favour of the latter through fear, even though nominally they should be on the side of the people.

The great day dawned. In the law court, three justiciars were seated at the dais table, and no fewer than four prominent lawyers representing Duke Henry. That man was not in court himself, possibly considering it below his dignity to seem to be countering some youngster from Scotland. Charles of Lorraine, Duke of Mayenne, was present, no doubt with a watching brief.

Thomas was encouraged when, just before the hearing started, an elderly man came up to him and declared that he was Eugène de Tott, a cousin of the young man's mother. He, and others of his family, were much in favour of Thomas's cause, although they were anxious not openly to offend the ducal cause. Almost all the people of Dieppe were of that mind, he assured, but dared not announce it.

Much heartened for his endeavours, Thomas bowed to the justiciars, and awaited the proceedings. Near by sat the Duke of Mayenne, a stern-looking personage.

It was that man who more or less took charge. Loftily he waved to the Guise lawyers.

One of these rose, to announce that Duke Henry's right to sell the harbour-dues of Dieppe had been wrongfully challenged, by the claim that these belonged to the city, not to the ducal dynasty. This false allegation demanded but little rebuttal; however, it was understood that there was present a foreigner, from Scotland, who asserted otherwise. The court was asked to pass judgment.

The central of the three justices inclined his head, and asked who contested the ducal rights.

Thomas rose, and was aware of the indrawn breaths of many at the obvious youthfulness of the protester.

He announced carefully that he came in the name of many of the people, without actually naming the Dieppe municipal authority; but also in the cause of certain Guise kin, including James Stewart, King of Scots.

That last drew still deeper breaths, and ensured attention.

Thomas, with every appearance of confidence, went on. He declared that the deep-water port of Dieppe, and its harbour-dues, was not all Guise property, although the land around, Béthune, and some of the city sites themselves, did belong to the ducal house. So they might claim some proportion of its earnings – but only a small proportion. The representatives of the citizens themselves – magistrates, merchants, trade-guilds, shipbuilders, dock-owners – held much greater claim to its dues. This was recognised by James, King of Scots, himself grandson of Queen Marie of Guise and son of Mary, Queen of Scots. It was firstly in King James's name that he now appeared.

The Duke of Mayenne snorted.

The spokesman of the three justices pointed at Thomas. What was his claim in this matter, as representing the King of Scotland – or saying that he did?

Thomas said that he had King James's personal instructions, as a Guise representative. But also that he desired and elected to speak on behalf of the good citizens of this Dieppe, of which his own mother, Jaqueline de Tott, had been one. His concession that Duke Henry and his kin held *some* right to the harbour-dues, but only a modest proportion, nowise invalidated his claim that King James did likewise, along with the greater rights of the people of the city and area. He also spoke on their behalf.

How could he, a young man from distant Scotland, speak for the people of Dieppe? he was asked.

It was not as himself that he spoke, he asserted, but for the cause of French law, with which he was conversant. The citizenry had their rights, as well as the landowners, and were represented by the mayor and magistrates and councillors. None could lawfully dispute that. Acts of the French Estates-General and parliament confirmed that, dating back as far as four centuries. He could so quote, if necessary.

There was a distinct pause as the justices eyed each other, glanced towards Mayenne, and back at Thomas.

He took his chance. In the circumstances, he went on, King James felt that an amicable settlement should be made on this of the harbour-dues, after the costs of collecting them were met. Two-thirds should remain with the municipality of Dieppe, and the remaining one-third be divided among the Guise family, not only Duke Henry – and here Thomas glanced at Mayenne. One-tenth should come to the King of Scots. That was His Grace's proposal, he, Thomas Hope, his representative.

This direct involvement of King James, of course, much concerned all there. Apart from his Guise blood, his mother had been Queen of France, as well as of Scots. The two-thirds proportion proposed for the city itself would find approval with the justiciars, even if they dared not acclaim it; but even the remaining one-third would be no mean sum to be divided among the Guises and James, Dieppe, the busiest port in northern France, ensuring that – and this an ongoing income.

Even Mayenne appeared to be calculating.

The justices declared that they would retire for a short time, to consider this suggestion.

Thomas felt reasonably confident. He saw the duke eyeing him assessingly, but did not seek to address him.

The justiciars were not away for long. When they returned, their spokesman announced that they had considered well, and decided that the suggested division of the dues, in King James's name, was fair and honest, this of the royal authority clearly of major worth to them. They would so recommend, to the mayor of Dieppe, the Masters of the Guilds, the representatives of Holy Church which was in some fashion concerned, and of course to Duke Henry of Guise, represented here by the Duke of Mayenne. Did he have any comment to add?

That man smoothed his chin, but said nothing.

So it was accepted, with sighs of relief all around, even Mayenne looking not displeased; after all, one-third represented a substantial sum of money. Thomas's assessment of the situation, as well as of the amounts involved, had been judicious.

He found himself being quietly congratulated thereafter, not actually by Mayenne but not criticised either, his use of the royal sanction effective, as had been his advocacy.

Young Thomas Hope's name would not be forgotten in Dieppe. As indication thereof, he found himself being made a burgess of Dieppe for his contribution, as his father was, likewise. This must have been an unusual distinction for one who had not yet graduated from the law school of St Mary's College of Edinburgh.

2

On his way home to Scotland, Thomas passed his eighteenth birthday on the ship, no celebrations involved, although the crew, Dieppe men themselves, hailed him as a burgess of their city now.

When he arrived back at Todd's Close, off the Castlehill of Edinburgh, it made a sad homecoming, for he learned that his father had died two weeks earlier, and had been interred in the family burial-ground at Greyfriars. Thither he went, there and then, to pay his respects, and to reassure himself that his parents would now be reunited. So he need not mourn for his sire, but only for himself and young brother Harry, whom he found to be in the care of their Uncle Edward, a rather stern and elderly man, and prominent in the Kirk.

Thomas's being made a burgess of Dieppe, and the prominence he had gained there, made no great impact in Edinburgh. But when, a couple of days later, he rode on one of his uncle's garrons the thirty-five miles west to Stirling, he did receive some interest and even commendation from his monarch.

King James was setting out for Falkland, in Fife, his favoured hunting-seat, and Thomas rode with him. The king was pleased to learn that he was to get some moneys from the Dieppe harbour-dues, demanding just how much, when, and whether there would be back-payments for years past – the Wisest Fool in Christendom was like that.

Thomas could not promise him the last, but assured that hereafter the mayor and magistrates thereof would send a tithe of their emoluments, as his royal share, and in appreciation of his monarchial backing. He told Thomas that he had done none so badly, for a bit laddie, and he would have to see how he could reward him someways.

"D'you ken Tam o' the Coogate?" he asked. "That's Hamilton o' Binning. He's the Lord Advocate, mind. He mebbe could gie you a bit help. In this o' the law. I'll hae a bit word wi' him."

"Until I have graduated, Sire, I am no full lawyer. That will be in just over a year's time."

"For a hauf-bakit lawman you did nane sae badly! This o' the Dieppe dues proves it. I'll can use you, whiles, methinks."

"I will be honoured, Sire."

"Yon Edward Hope – he's your uncle, no? A right hard yin him, I'm tell't. But he maun be getting auld, for he was close to John Knox, and *he's* been deid a score o' years. He was a commissioner to the first General Assembly o' the Kirk, I mind. They say he aided at the slaying o' yon Rizzio man."

"As to that, I know not, Your Grace. But, yes, he is my uncle. As are Alexander, a tailor; and James, also a lawyer."

"Aye – and Petit John Trumpet? Whae was he? Kin o' yours? He was trumpeter to my great-grandsire, if I mind richt."

"Yes, Sire. Trumpeter at the court of King James the Fourth. He was called Petit, or Little, John because he was so big a man. He was wounded at Flodden-field, when the king died, but survived."

"You Hopes are a right acquart lot! *You've* done weel, though, wi' this o' Dieppe. I'm thinking that I can mak use o' you. Aye, in this o' the Kirk lands and the reformers. It's a right tangle as to the law o' it a'. Tam Hamilton kens it a', the law. But I could dae wi' some ither advising in this o' the law, see you. In the matter o' lands, in especial. The auld Romish Kirk had great lands. Lords and lairds hae been dying, doon the centuries; and getting auld, they began tae consider whither their souls were bound! And sae left land to the priests, for prayers to be said for them ever after!

"But the crown, see you, had, and has, its rights ower a' the land, temporalities you lawmen ca' it, feudal dues ower and above lairdly yins, vassalage, fiefs and the like. I'm King o' Scotland, mind, as weel as king o' Scots. Superior o' a' the land. A' the lairds had to swear fealty to me at my coronation, a foot on the soil frae a' their lands. But the Romish priests didna. *They* held their lands frae God, they said. But since this o' reform, it's no' the same. The lords hae fought ower and gotten the lands. And *I'm* due my dues. Yon temporalities. I'm no' getting it a'. And Tam Hamilton's a laird himsel'. For his Binning and Drumcairn. He's gotten himsel' cried Lord Drumcairn, a Lord o' Session. Aye, and mair than that. Laird o' Byres o' Garleton, Barnbougle, Monkland and Dalmeny. Ooh, aye – I hae been watching that yin! *He's* no' for paying mair temporalities and fealties and crown dues than he maun. Sae he's for letting ithers off, tae. You tak me? But *you're* nae laird. Sae you can gie me the richt advice I need in this o' the law. Surer than Hamilton."

"If I can, it will be my pleasure, Sire."

"You fair ootwitted thae Guise dukes, raivelled them! You can dae the same for fowk who would ootwit mysel'! This o' the auld Kirk's lands. All o' them. Consider you these, a' ower my kingdom. Look close. And tell me. I'll see that you dinna suffer for it. Dae that, Hope man."

"As you will, Sire. But – it will take some time."

"Ooh, aye. I'll can wait . . ."

So Thomas had a task, a major task on his hands, to discover the great and widespread lands that Holy Church had garnered down the centuries, and try to trace most of the present owners, after the Reformation, or at least the major ones. The king's mother, Mary, Queen of Scots, and his grandmother, Queen Marie of Guise, being strong Catholics, had not pursued this quest. But James Stewart was otherwise – and Thomas had to be his faithful subject. He would have to watch, however, not to get too far wrong with this Hamilton, Lord of Session Drumcairn, so powerful in matters of law; and this before he himself had so much as graduated. Caution was called for, as well as initiative and legal skills.

This of the king's charge, to identify the Catholic Church's lands throughout the kingdom, would keep him busy indeed meantime, for it would be a huge undertaking, calling for his visiting and enquiring into every lordship, lairdship, county, region, diocese and parish of the land, a mammoth endeavour. But it was by way of being a royal command. As well that he was his own master, as regards time, and had a sufficiency of moneys, left him by his mother in especial, for King James had made no mention of paying him, save to say that he would not suffer for it. This monarch was notably tight-fisted. But he might well be repaid in other ways than in gold and silver coin.

Thomas set about planning his mission. At least he had a sturdy garron to carry him on it.

To visit every corner of Scotland would have to be done methodically and over a lengthy period, he recognised. It was *lands* that had to be identified, rather than communities, cities, towns and villages, although these would have to be considered where ownership was concerned. Most of Lothian Thomas knew well, so that could be left until the final summing up. Where to start, then? He decided on the Merse, the eastern Borderland up to where this linked with the eastern end of the Lammermuir Hills, especially as it contained the great Church lands of the abbeys of Melrose, Dryburgh and Kelso, and numerous priories, such as Coldinghame, Ladykirk, Polwarth and Eccles.

Thither he rode, and quickly perceived something of the vastness of the duty that King James had laid upon him. Until he commenced it he had had only the faintest realisation of what was involved, how much land there was to survey, how many lords, lairds, farmers and millers, not to mention flock-masters, shepherds and fishermen, to gain the overall picture required. The king had raised one eyebrow when he said that he could wait. Had *he* had some notion of what it involved?

Days passed into weeks and weeks into months, while Thomas explored in depth the Borderland, its East, Middle and West Marches, Dumfries-shire, great Galloway, Ayrshire, Lanarkshire, Glasgow and the Clyde estuary lands. The notes and details he drew up grew into great bundles and volumes; and still he journeyed and examined, interviewed and questioned. Fife followed, and then Perthshire and up into Aberdeenshire and the Highlands, all on his liege-lord's behalf; he found it highly interesting for its own sake, challenging, even though he was by no means always popular among the lordly ones, and even the clerics. All such were fairly thorough at collecting their feudal dues, but less good at passing on those royal temporalities. Thomas's reminders were often far from welcome. He had no instructions nor obligations to do so, only to gather the information; but he felt it only fair to his monarch.

Studies at the law school inevitably suffered in all this, although Thomas did seek to keep up with his learning progress to ensure that he passed the strict requirements of his mentors at the college for graduation, much-thumbed legal papers being carried in his over-full satchel along with the seemingly endless notes he was taking anent the land ownership situation. And now the final graduation examinations were almost upon him.

It seemed strange, after all his visiting and peregrinations, to be sitting, that early spring of 1592, at the law school of St Mary's College, this part of the new University of Edinburgh, founded only nine years before, a mere pupil and student, however experienced in aspects of his chosen profession. He passed his tests and interrogations with fair ease, needless to say, possibly his Uncle Edward's renown and prominence not hindering in this. He was accepted for graduation, and ordered to complete his practical inauguration thereto as a clerk to James Nicolson, Writer, a partner of his Uncle James, at his premises in Brown's Close. Fortunately his new master there accepted Thomas as already fully qualified, and indeed skilled in his craft, his association with King James much spoken of, so that this of matriculation was more or less taken for granted.

Thomas could now rightfully call himself lawyer, aged nineteen. He continued with his legal studies, however, when he could find the time to do so. He now sought to advance to the higher status of advocate, a member of the faculty whose members could plead before the High Court of Scotland – not that he had any intention meantime so to do, but for the authority that it would give him in law.

Thomas Hope was a busy young man indeed. He re-

cognised, of course, his advantages, in his family background, his links with the monarch, and his part in the
Dieppe dispute, the which was now well known in Scotland
on account of the impact on merchant-traders, especially
from Leith, and its significant financial effects. His profi-
ciency in the French language and law was also of profit.
Many of the Edinburgh and Leith merchants who dealt
with the Continent called on his assistance in their affairs.

But all the time, this of the king's remit to survey the
former Church lands was his principal preoccupation, so
huge a task was it. Some had already changed hands from
the reformist gainers, some had become divided up, and not
all the new lairds were readily contacted, absent. And with
the whole of Scotland to cover, Thomas was faced with an
ongoing duty of all but endless duration and complexity.
He did not exactly curse King James for the requirement,
for the undertaking was highly interesting and informative,
but he did find it overmuch. And he had to make constant
reports to the monarch, who had to be reached at various
locations, Stirling, Falkland, Holyrood, Dumbarton or
wherever, this often entailing much enquiry and back-
tracking.

On one such interview, or audience as the king termed it,
Thomas did raise the issue. "This prospecting of the entire
realm, Sire, is a mighty mission for one man. I have learned
that there are over thirteen hundred parishes in your kingdom, this not counting the Hebridean and Orkney and
Shetland isles. It is almost too much to achieve alone. Could
Your Grace not engage some others to assist in this?"

"Aye, I could, man. But it wouldna be the same. *You* ken
what I want and what you're at. Ithers wouldna dae it the
same way, gie me the same view, cover a' the ground. It's *ae*
man's charge, and *you're* my man in this. I want *ae* picture,

no' a wheen o' them, different. And the ithers would hae to ken the law – and maist lawyers, I've found, are no' like you! They're ower apt to be auld, crabbit, wi' their nebs deep in papers. You'll dae for me – and you'll no' regret it, I've tell't you."

"As you will, Sire. But it will be a lengthy undertaking."

"You're young enough to dae it, and tae finish it, man. Seven years younger than mysel', I'm tell't. See you tae it, man Hope."

So that was that.

3

Thomas's survey was direly interrupted shortly thereafter. The Earl of Moray, handsome and debonair, a favourite of James's queen, Anne of Denmark, and a Protestant leader, was foully murdered at his Donibristle seat in West Fife by the Earl of Huntly, these two lords having long been at feud. It had been a gruesome slaying indeed; Huntly had attacked Donibristle Castle by night and, in order to get Moray and his attendants out, had piled brushwood against the mouths of the drainage flues which led down through the thickness of the walling to discharge the effluent from the garderobes on the upper floors, a sanitary development. Set ablaze, the smoke from these fires, drawn up, rendered the stronghold untenable, and the defenders had to seek to make their escape. Most were slain as they did so, the darkness lit up by the flames. The earl himself, perceiving this, elected to lower himself by a rope from an upper window at the rear. Unfortunately he landed among the all but continuous fire along the walling-foot, and, of all mishaps, his long hair caught fire. Running off thus ablaze, and pausing to pull his doublet over his head to quench the flames, he was seen and caught up with by Huntly's men, and smitten down. In this attack he was slashed across the face by one of the Gordons, with a dagger, and the other earl coming up, seeing it, protested that the slashing should have been done by himself, as suitable, and, drawing his own dirk, added his own stab at the bleeding features.

"Curse you, Huntly – you have spoiled a better face than your own!" the assaulted man gasped.

Thus died the Bonnie Earl o' Moray, to be sung about throughout the land thereafter.

Thomas heard rumours that King James had urged Huntly on to this murder, this because of his queen's known fondness and admiration for the victim.

Huntly being so prominent a Catholic and Moray a Protestant, this deed sparked off an escalation of fierce religious animosity, and King James was advised to call a parliament to seek to damp it down. Thomas himself had no role to play thereat, but went to watch the proceedings from the gallery of the Great Hall of Edinburgh Castle.

It made a tumultuous and bitter session, needless to say. Scotland was now mainly Protestant, of course, and the great majority present were of that persuasion. Huntly remained discreetly absent, but his friends and colleagues, the Catholic Earls of Angus and Errol, were there, and spoke up in his favour, although they were outvoted on all points.

A telling factor against the Catholics was brought out. One of their messengers, a George Kerr, had been apprehended bearing a letter addressed to the King of Spain. This was blank, unworded, but signed by Huntly, Angus and Errol. The man Kerr, interrogated under torture, had confessed that, once safely out of Scotland, he was to write in the wording, this to urge that a Spanish fleet should sail up the Highland west coast – the Highlanders being mainly still Catholic – to coincide with a rising in those parts, led by the three earls. This of the Spanish Blanks, as it came to be called, became an important factor not only for that parliament but for the nation as a whole.

The session passed four decrees, by a large majority. Catholic clerics were no longer to be allowed to vote in parliament, with Episcopalian bishops only allowed to attend. Kirk ministers were to stamp out all Catholic "heresies" in their parishes. And nationally no Catholic worship, especially the Mass, was to be countenanced, even at dead of night. Finally, all Catholic priests and students were to leave the capital, and other cities, forthwith.

The king later confessed to Thomas that he was distinctly doubtful as to the fairness and wisdom of some of this, he himself, although Protestant, believing in freedom of worship. But the parliamentary majority was strong in favour, and Moray's murder a notable instigation. Scotland was to remain vehemently reformed.

To emphasise this, Angus there present was arrested and sent to be confined elsewhere in Edinburgh Castle indefinitely, although Errol managed to make his escape when he saw the way matters were going.

Thomas, having had a Catholic mother, and with his French connections and interests, was not fiercely Protestant, and deplored all the controversy, holding, like his monarch, that men and women should be free to worship their Creator in their own way. But he was interested in the debate, if such it could be called, and in the passions it aroused.

There were repercussions, for the parliament advised – it could not command – the monarch to demonstrate that he ruled a Protestant realm, this to the Highlanders, not only the Gordons and their allies. Moreover Elizabeth Tudor sent £3,000 to encourage him to do so, and this had to be positively acknowledged. She also offered him six thousand armed men to emphasise the matter, but this he hastily refused. He would provide his own supporters. And the powerful Earl of Atholl produced twelve hundred foot and nine hundred horse to add to the royal force.

Thomas was ordered to accompany this major army northwards, as being expert in his knowledge of every corner of the land; so he found himself riding among the commanders and clan chiefs at the head of the array, no warrior as he might be. At least he was able to advise on routes and point out features not generally known to his companions, including the monarch.

They went from Stirling by the Allan Water and Auchterarder into Strathearn and so to Perth, where the monarch was received by the provost and magistrates with much acclaim. Then on by Forfar and down Strathmore, picking up the contingents of Protestant nobles, so that, halting overnight at the Bishop of Brechin's palace, by the time they reached Aberdeen the company had swollen to twice its original size. Huntly and his associates, unable to match this great host, fled north to Caithness-shire.

Reaching Inverness eventually, James decided that this was sufficient. There he declared the Catholic earls forfeited and their estates to become crown property – although this was only a gesture, the fulfilling of which would have been all but impossible. Indeed the king advisedly behaved leniently towards the lands and the people, even allowing the Countess of Huntly to remain in her Bog o' Gight castle unassailed.

Thomas, enjoying a fairly close relationship with the monarch, much approved of this clement attitude, although some of the lords declared it weak and inexpedient. But James Stewart, no warlike despot, saw himself as father of his people, however odd a one, and sought to have them loyal to himself, personally, even if many of his nobles might see it otherwise.

The royal array remained at Inverness, this scarcely to the satisfaction of the citizenry, who had to put up with the invasion and all that entailed to their cost, more especially towards their young women. James went hunting deer in the nearby mountains, which Thomas judged a suitable reaction, no word of major uprising coming from Catholic sympathisers. In these circumstances the army gradually dispersed, as lords perceived no point in remaining mobilised, especially with the harvest upon them and their levies concerned with the ingathering.

It might all amount to an anticlimax, but their liege-lord preferred it that way, whatever Elizabeth Tudor thought as to the results of her £3,000 gift in the Protestant cause. Thomas for one applauded, although his Uncle Edward did not.

James did consult the younger man on this matter of the parliamentary forfeiture of Huntly's and the others' lands. What did the law say as to the like?

Thomas pointed out that parliament was not above the law, unless it specifically passed an Act, later endorsed by the Lords of the Articles, abrogating the legal limitations in this matter. It had not done so, as yet. The Catholic lords and Highland chiefs could claim immunity in law.

Their unusual liege-lord decided to follow his preferred reaction to so many issues, and do nothing. He ordered a turnabout, to head back for Stirling.

Thomas was becoming somewhat concerned for his young brother Harry, now in his twenty-second year. Under his stern Uncle Edward's supervision he was fretting, not enjoying being a clerk in the Leith office. If Thomas, at his age, had been able to fare far afield, even to the Continent, why not he? His brother felt slightly guilty. Their father had told him to look after Harry. That brother was very different from himself, lacking much in the way of initiative, and hitherto content to accept life as it came. But now he was stirring, with no especial aims but desiring escape from a clerk's desk, for which Thomas by no means blamed him. He had not studied law, nor anything else of practical value. What was he to do about Harry?

In the midst of these wonderings, a royal situation developed in which Thomas became involved. The king had long been afraid of witchcraft, deeming such responsible for various mishappenings, including the occasion when, returning to Scotland with his bride, Anne of Denmark, he claimed that he had seen witches, in the form of hares, rowing a small boat around his ship, this as a threat against him by the devil – rather typically James Stewart. As a result he had initiated a campaign against witchcraft, many women being accused of it, especially on the claims of hostile or jealous neighbours. Witch trials were becoming frequent, the monarch ordering these to take place before himself, largely at North Berwick on the Haddingtonshire coast, offshore of which James had allegedly seen the hares rowing their boat – although no one else had seen them. Now he was gaining confessions from accused women, this by having leather belts tightly buckled around their brows, and a dirk inserted between leather and skin and twisted, so as to lift off flesh and hair, the unfortunates, needless to say, thus persuaded to admit almost anything. And this in the name of the law.

Thomas was greatly distressed by it all, and sought to use what influence he had with his liege-lord to halt it. He asserted that in fact there was no law passed against witchcraft, sorcery and so-called black magic; and until there might be, such punishments upon alleged practitioners were unlawful. The king rejected this counsel, and a rift developed between monarch and a favoured subject, Thomas claiming that James's declared wish to act as a father to his people was being undermined by this behaviour. The consequent coolness resulted in Thomas's retiral from the royal court. Fortunately his survey of the former Church lands was all but complete, and its findings left with his uncles to transmit to the king.

In the circumstances Thomas decided that it might be expedient to absent himself from Scotland for a spell, and to tackle a project that had been at the back of his mind for some time. This was to take further advantage of his family links not only with Dieppe but with the Low Countries as a whole, and use his knowledge of international law, as well as his burgess-ship, to some effect. Amsterdam rivalled Dieppe and Hamburg as the greatest commercial port in all Europe, and if he could use such abilities as he had there, and thence to Hamburg and the Hanseatic League's base at Lübeck near by, on the Baltic, who knew what might result? And he would take his brother Harry with him, get him away from Uncle Edward.

So the pair found a ship, at Leith, to transport them to the Low Countries, Harry much excited.

Amsterdam, situated where the River Amstel entered the Zuider Zee, that great inland sea, was one of the largest cities Thomas had ever seen, a huge commercial port trading with the East in especial, Africa and the Indies, rich, the importing of diamonds being notable, all but a monopoly. It was indeed this last that attracted Thomas thither, it having occurred to him that if an actual monopoly could be established this could prove to be an enormous advantage to that city. Could such be contrived? Lawfully? What conditions were required to gain a monopoly? He rather thought that it was possible. In which case it could be highly profitable to all concerned, to say the least.

He consulted Amsterdam lawyers. He was no Dutch speaker, but French was all but a second language in the Netherlands, and he had no difficulty in learning what he desired. This was, as he had anticipated, that a monopoly could only be established by the formation of an association, a company, with governmental authority, and unless this establishment was copied by other states' government it would only apply to the one nation. But if the import of diamonds was already more or less based on Amsterdam, from Africa, the Indies and elsewhere, it ought to be possible to regularise the monopoly by law, international law, and so create a most notable source of wealth for the Netherlands. Why had this not been done?

His enquiries brought forth no real enlightenment. It seemed to have been no one's concern, with the diamond trade being already more or less confined to Amsterdam. But, surely, it would be only a question of time before the possibilities were perceived, the demand for diamonds growing, not only for jewellery and adornment but for sundry practical uses, because diamonds were the hardest substance known on earth. This could be worth looking into, using his status as a Scots lawyer who had gained fame over the Dieppe harbour-dues issue. So – some sort of association?

He conferred with the burgomaster of Amsterdam, and through him with two members of the States-General, the government, on this of a monopoly, and aroused some interest and speculation. It was agreed that if it could be contrived, undoubtedly it would be highly profitable.

Thomas's enquiries elicited the fact that Antwerp, some seventy-five miles to the south, all but rivalled Amsterdam in the import of diamonds. That city was a great port, at the head of the longest estuary in western Europe, into which flowed the River Schelde. He would visit Antwerp, and discover how the diamond trade featured there. This of diamonds was becoming ever more prominent in Thomas's thinking.

There was no problem in finding a vessel to take him and Harry to Antwerp, by Veere, with its Scottish associations, and the Wester Schelde estuary. It proved to be a very large city, allegedly with no fewer than one hundred thousand inhabitants, with breweries, distilleries, clothing and tapestry factories, bleaching works and, to be sure, diamond-polishing mills. Here was the ambience he sought.

There Thomas put to the wealthy diamond merchants his theories of a shared monopoly with Amsterdam for the trade in the precious stones, forming a company or association to attain their governments' agreement to control between them this lucrative activity, cornering the entire European market. He found the dealers doubtful at first, but when he persuaded the burgomaster of Antwerp to co-operate with his opposite number at Amsterdam, the battle was all but won. An association to control a diamond monopoly was to be established.

Thomas had it all thought out, the contacts to be sought in distant lands, the go-betweens, the shippers to be trusted with such valuable merchandise, the payments to be made depending on the size and quality – for diamonds could vary, like other substances. He even had a name for the association to be established, the East India Company, which style would cover a great area of the producing territories, from Africa to China.

So be it.

4

All this convincing, arranging and establishing took a considerable time, with much travelling involved, and it was the new century before the East India Company's formation was agreed upon, and the quite lengthy process of setting it up was completed. Meanwhile, back in Scotland, Thomas had been admitted to the Faculty of Advocates, although he had not begun to practise at the bar, being over-busy elsewhere. In fact, he was in the strange position of being well known, all but famous, on the Continent, but not in his own native land, the Scots being but little concerned with such ornamental and superfluous objects as diamonds, its nobility rich in lands rather than in money, and its prosperous merchants having more to do with their gold and silver than invest in diamonds for their womenfolk's adornment. And, of course, he was seldom now in Scotland for any lengthy periods. The formation of the East India Company had, as yet, little impact there.

Rather strangely, it was his relationship with his distinctly odd monarch that resulted in Thomas Hope's name becoming known in his homeland, for James was interested in this of diamonds, not for themselves but over the wealth that could be generated therefrom – because he had inherited an all but empty treasury, and was having marked difficulty in refilling it. Anything that could bring in revenues was highly welcome, and he saw some involvement in a diamond monopoly as valuable. Not that he was in any position to invest in diamond dealing, too costly a proceeding to embark on; but he could use Thomas to deal on his behalf in a small way by gaining a few shares in the East India Company, in Thomas's name so that no note of it need appear in the royal revenue records, a private and very useful arrangement – and one that ensured Thomas's ready access to the royal presence at any time. Queen Elizabeth Tudor, now aged sixty-seven, was not in the best of health, and it seemed probable that James, her heir through the marriage of Henry the Eighth's sister, Margaret Tudor, to James the Fourth, his great-grandfather, would succeed to the English throne before long, and hopefully be in a position to invest more actively, with the improved fortunes anticipated.

Meantime the strange king could bind Thomas closer to the royal cause by having him appointed Solicitor, Advocate and Procurator to the Church of Scotland. Sir Thomas Hamilton of Priestfield and Binning, the Lord Advocate, was ambitious, desirous of becoming a *real* lord, not just Lord of Session Drumcairn, and was seeking to be created an earl, hopefully Earl of Melrose, he having purchased the valuable abbey revenues there, which had become available at the Reformation. He probably could be persuaded to yield up this position of Procurator to the Kirk of Scotland to Thomas, and the appointment be ratified by Uncle Edward Hope, who had been Lord High Commissioner to the Church of Scotland and remained powerful in the General Assembly. As an official position this could be useful to Thomas, although he was no Kirk zealot.

As it transpired, this relationship with Tam o' the Coogate, as the king termed Hamilton, whose handsome residence was in that lengthy thoroughfare of the capital leading from the Grassmarket below the castle to the royal hunting-forest, known as the King's Park, the Cowgate, brought Thomas in touch with an interesting, notable and very useful character, George Heriot, the monarch's usurer or banker, known as Jinglin' Geordie because of his wealth. James was ever in debt to Heriot, and saw this of the diamonds as being one possible way out of his financial difficulties. Thomas got on well with Heriot, who was a cousin of Hamilton's, the latter's mother having been Elizabeth Heriot, daughter of a small laird, that of Trabroun in Haddingtonshire.

This of the diamonds, needless to say, much attracted Jinglin' Geordie, who saw the possibilities of further financial gain through the East India Company, and was prepared to purchase shares therein, and, if so desired, lend Thomas money on favourable terms to do the same. Another useful relationship came about.

So Thomas and Harry returned to Amsterdam to continue with some part in the development of the East India Company, which was extending far beyond the matter of diamonds.

They found King James's interest and support welcomed for more than his promised contribution. The Spanish threat was worrying the company, for Spain had the greatest navy in all the world, and the East Indies were very vulnerable to such. All anti-Spanish backing was to be valued. The spice trade was becoming important, and the Spanish ships a menace to that.

The brothers learned that the Dutch government had declared a trade monopoly for all the area between the Cape of Good Hope eastwards to the Straits of Magellan, at the tip of South America, this of course including the East Indies, and was intent on establishing colonies in such as Sumatra, Java, Madura and Borneo, despite the ancient

Chinese influence there. How would the Spaniards and Portuguese react to this? Warfare on the seas could grievously damage trade, and for more than the East India Company. Thomas was concerned, as indeed were loftier folk in the Low Countries. King James would probably be so likewise. Why could not the nations respect each other's interests and remain at peace?

Harry, now in his twenty-fourth year, surprised his brother by announcing that he intended to remain in Amsterdam. He had decided to build on the interest in diamonds, and to set up a diamond-polishing mill, such as they had seen at Antwerp. Thomas could not object to this, although he would much miss him. Todd's Close would seem a very empty house hereafter.

Back home there, it so happened that he found himself placed in a difficult position, as the new Procurator of the Church of Scotland. For the Kirk was still preoccupied with putting down witchcraft, which seemed to be on the increase, for some reason. Thomas much deplored this campaign against the women, and recognised how easy it was for ill-wishers to accuse others of the offence, and how difficult for the innocent to contest the charges, since almost anything that a woman might be concerned with, which was not a general custom, could be construed as a leaning towards witchcraft. For instance, an interest in medicinal herbs, a fondness for cats, the ancient practice of hanging pieces of cloth at holy wells for good fortune, alleged communication with the dead, and lone pursuits and preferences could be used to condemn; and of course the king's known concern with and fear of sorcery did not help.

A former friend of his late father, a small laird named Bennett of Wallyford, this near the town of Musselburgh, came to Thomas, as a lawyer, to defend one of his female servants accused of witchcraft, an awkward request in the circumstances. But he felt that, in all honesty, he could not refuse; and it would be an opportunity to seek to counter the growing trend for witch-hunting. It might well widen the slight rift with his liege-lord, which was unfortunate; but the issue was quite important, he felt.

Enquiries revealed that a young woman from Tranent in Haddingtonshire had been seen by two elderly neighbours running and skipping alone around a little lochan on the Gledsmuir, between Tranent and Haddington, where they had gone to pick brambles. This much shocked the viewers, for the girl was naked, presumably having been bathing, who declared that it could only be sinful witchery. They reported it to their parish minister, who informed the local presbytery, whose members, knowing of King James's preoccupation with witch trials, sent word to the monarch. James ordered the young woman, Isobel Grieve by name, to appear before him at the harbour chapel of North Berwick, scene of previous witch trials.

Thomas went to consult John Bennett at Wallyford, where he learned that the accused was the personal servant of the laird's daughter, Elizabeth, who was much upset by the situation. For she was fond of this Isobel, declaring that any charges of witchcraft were ridiculous, and that she herself had sometimes gone to bathe and swim in the lochan with the girl. Indignant against the accusers, she had urged her father to seek out a good advocate to fight the case.

Thomas was not hard to convince of the innocence of the young woman, the more so in that he was struck by the good looks and strong advocacy of Elizabeth Bennett, a lively creature of dark hair, lustrous eyes, friendly nature and excellent figure. He pointed out the king's strange antipathy towards witchcraft, and was led to agree to do what he could to gain the girl's acquittal, the charge unfounded.

Elizabeth took him to see the accused in a cottage on the property where she lived with her widowed mother, her late father having been a shepherd. She proved to be a sonsy, buxom girl, against whom any allegation of witchcraft seemed absurd.

The two young women pointed out that the lochan, at Woodside on the Back Burn of Letham, was an excellent place for swimming, private, amid birches and copseland, where seemingly roe-deer frequently came to drink. The two accusing bramble-pickers must have been in some way inimical towards this Isobel or her mother.

Thomas got on well with Elizabeth Bennett, an outgoing character who announced herself to be interested in his activities, especially his challenging of the ducal Guises and the Dieppe controversy while so young a man. It had become a famous case, even in Scotland, and she had assumed that the victor had been a senior and much older lawyer, not someone of about her own age. He decided that he must see more of this Elizabeth. He told her that the next time she was in Edinburgh she should call in at his office at the house in Todd's Close, where he would show her sundry objects that might well interest her, including the gold key he had won with his burgess-ship of Dieppe; the like status in Edinburgh did not rise to any such symbol, merely a page of parchment.

Elizabeth took his invitation sufficiently seriously to visit Todd's Close one week later, and much appreciated all that he had to show her. She retaliated by saying that he must come to Wallyford House, when she would take him to view the pool on Gledsmuir where Isobel Grieve had attracted the attention of those two bramble-pickers. They might well see roe-deer.

He said that he would look forward to that.

He was not disappointed. On a warm August day they rode the eight miles from Wallyford, skirting Tranent and Macmerry, and on to Gledsmuir on the road to Haddington, to turn off southwards towards the Lammermuir foothills in the vicinity of a farm called Hopefield, which had Thomas wondering whether it had had anything to do with his family. Soon thereafter, in open woodland, they came to their lochan destination, and sure enough they twice glimpsed roe-deer slipping off among the birch trees. The pool, really only a brief widening of the Back Burn, was an attractive and secluded location where any bather might expect to be private – save perhaps from the eyes of berry-pickers in August.

"No place for the practice of witchcraft!" Thomas commented. "I much like it here."

"It is a favourite spot of mine. I am often here to swim, in summer. It was myself who first brought Isobel here. Carrying her pillion on my horse. It is a deal nearer, and more private, than the seashore at Gosford or Aberlady Bay."

"I must remember that, next time I feel disposed to swim! Who knows the company I might have!"

She gazed at him, one eyebrow raised. "You prefer a companion at your swimming?"

"Well, if I had the choice! A, a suitable companion! I enjoy swimming. But in Edinburgh I do not get much of it."

"So we might expect you *here*, on occasion?" She added, "With a friend?"

"Unless I could find that suitable companion hereabouts. As . . . guide!"

"Ah! Well, we might find you the like, Master Thomas. If so required."

"I will hold you to that, Mistress Elizabeth! One of these warm days, if this fine weather continues."

"Who knows? Perhaps you ought to take the chance, while it lasts?"

"And this of companion?"

She did not answer that. "When is Isobel Grieve to appear before the king on this foolish charge of witch-craft?"

"I do not know. The king is at Falkland meantime. He said that he would have her tried at his favoured witchcraft venue of North Berwick. I will be glad to defend the lass, if necessary. Indeed I will urge him not to go ahead with this matter. As quite unnecessary. Do you know these two women who brought the charge?"

"No. Only that they come from Tranent."

"Could you find them for me? I would speak with them. See if this folly can be avoided, the matter disposed of, without the king being involved. It is all so foolish, point-less, to be involving the monarch. James is obsessed with this of witchcraft."

"That would be best, yes. I will seek the women out for you."

"And soon? So that we can keep the king out of it, if possible."

"Give me one day, to find them."

Two days later Thomas was back at Wallyford House, where Elizabeth's father eyed him assessingly, but made no objection to him seeing his daughter. Elizabeth told him that she had identified the two women who had accused Isobel Grieve, and learned that they had long been the enemies of Christina Grieve, the girl's mother, and had conceived this method of assailing her. She had told them that a noted lawyer was concerned in the matter, and might well summon them to appear before the king if they did not admit to him, in front of witnesses, that they had acted out of malice. Alarmed, they had agreed to do so. She and her father would accompany Thomas to Tranent, to act as the necessary witnesses.

Another two days, and again at Tranent, the two women were much agitated to be faced by a lawyer and the laird of Wallyford, and made no bones about confessing that, yes, they had done what they had as a blow against the girl's mother Christina. Thomas had a statement written out, and the pair made their marks on this, neither being able to write, the witnesses adding their signatures. Thomas would have this sent on to the king at Falkland, and trust that it would see an end to the whole annoying affair, and Isobel Grieve be left in peace hereafter.

Thomas was, of course, all for holding Elizabeth to her suggestion of them both returning to that lochan on Gledsmuir. Elizabeth's father had no wish to go visiting places eight miles away, a man becoming frail. He left the two younger people to it.

It was a glorious August afternoon, and Thomas was delighted with the prospect and the company.

At the lochan, dismounting, and aiding Elizabeth down, he well recognised that this was an opportunity too good to miss.

"It is warm enough for a swim," he observed, as casually as he might. "Would you . . . care so to do?"

"Aha! I wondered if that might arise! But, why not? So long as there are no berry-pickers around to accuse us of witchcraft!"

"You do not object? Object to a man, naked? And yourself likewise? I can go to the far end of this pond, if so."

"Why should you? I have two brothers, both now married, whom I have often seen unclothed, as God made us. And no doubt you have seen women likewise, ere this. So long as it . . . goes no further!"

He bowed to her. "You have my word for it, madam."

"So – a gentleman! I judge myself to be safe!"

Tethering their horses to birch trees, despite her declarations, Elizabeth moved over to a convenient broom bush, behind which to undress. Thomas, shrugging, stripped off there on the shore.

He was in fact in the water, quite warm, before the young woman came running down to join him. She was quite excellently built, and clearly was not embarrassed by it being so obvious, at least on this occasion. He was duly appreciative.

They swam together, she twice deliberately splashing the water in his face, before turning over to float on her back. This he could never achieve, without doubling up and sinking. Were women made differently so that this was possible, more curves and buoyancy?

Thereafter they ran together round the lochan to dry off, a pleasing exercise for Thomas, who would have further continued the process by lying together in the sunshine. But Elizabeth went to her bush to re-dress herself when he indicated it, wagging a finger at him. Apparently enough was enough.

Presently she came back, fully clad, to lie also, but not over-close, and, strangely, he felt uncomfortable about this now, and went to dress. But he would not forget this afternoon.

When, presently, they returned to the horses, he declared

that this had been a highly enjoyable occasion. They must do it again.

She raised her expressive eyebrows. "Because we were both naked? It must not become a habit, my friend. Implying some consorting."

"I would not be against some consorting, Elizabeth!"

"Perhaps not. But we women must beware of the like, see you. If . . . over-frequent!"

He shrugged, and made a face.

They rode back to Wallyford.

5

This of the East India Company had Thomas returning to Amsterdam that autumn. This was because all investing therein, or having dealings therewith, were being required by the Dutch government to swear an oath of loyalty, on account of Spain's claims to parts of the Indies, although it had established no real colonies, only kept patrolling the seas there with its fleets. The company was becoming highly important and profitable, the spice trade in especial flourishing, overtaking that of the diamonds, sesame oil being found to be helpful in the treatment of diseases, as well as useful in wine-making, and peppers, ginger, nut-meg, cinnamon and vanilla much sought after. So the thriving company was being taken over by the Dutch government, and all investors' support demanded for the monopoly. Thomas had some shares, George Heriot had many, and even King James a few. So the visit to Amster-dam was called for. Also Thomas was anxious to discover how brother Harry was faring there, with rumours among the shipmen that he was prospering.

So he sought out a vessel at Leith to take him – not overlooking a farewell visit to Wallyford House, where he was urged to hasten back.

At Amsterdam he found much concern over the Spanish situation, indeed the Netherlands government considering whether to declare war on Spain over the raiding of its colonies in the Indies. Only the lack of warships was restraining it. The East India Company, needless to say vulnerable indeed, was in a state of anxiety, pressing for at least diplomatic support, and a rallying of all the rest of Europe against Spain. Thomas was able to convey King James's favour for this.

He found Harry doing very well, and making quite a name for himself, in Antwerp as well as Amsterdam, branching out into trading in spices, recognising the potential of links with the company. Diamonds had become of secondary importance to him. He was now a burgess, and aiming higher.

The brothers discussed this of the Spanish threat, and agreed that a united front of the nations against Spain was called for. Warships, of course, were the answer, but unfortunately only the Portuguese were strong enough in this respect openly to challenge the Spaniards; and Portugal, placed as it was and flanked by Spain, could readily be assailed by land as well as by sea by its larger neighbour. How to win over the Portuguese to action?

Pressure might be brought to bear on them by the Vatican. But, unfortunately or otherwise, the opposing nations were almost all Protestant while Spain was strongly Catholic. It occurred to Thomas that if the Catholic minorities in the anti-Spanish countries were to unite in appealing to the Pope to bring pressure, even the threat of national excommunication and stigma on its priesthood, this could be effective. How could it be achieved?

Harry had his links with Antwerp, now a burgess there also. Could he introduce Thomas to the archbishop there? To propose an alliance against Spain, and an appeal to the Vatican?

The brothers rode to Antwerp and were able to gain an interview with the archbishop. They found him predisposed towards them, for the country's trade and wellbeing were also suffering from the Spanish aggression. He agreed that an urgent request from the Catholics in the Protestant lands for papal condemnation of Spain's attacks would be of considerable value.

Thomas offered to make a tour round the reformed lands to advocate a united appeal by the Catholics therein against Spain; also to do what he could to convince the Protestant authorities to act together in the same cause.

Harry's spice trading involved him with the shipping interests at Amsterdam and Antwerp, and he was able to convince one of the wealthy owners to give them the use of a medium-sized vessel for a few weeks before the winter storms set in, this the *Chanson*. Aboard this the brothers set off on a series of visits to the Scandinavian, German, Baltic, English and Scottish capitals, making good use of King James's name and advocacy, adding thereto those of other rulers as they went, Thomas's own personal credit greatly aiding in their acceptance, allied to the ever increasing repute of the East India Company. Their progress was notably successful, thanks to the continuing piratical activities of the Spanish ships; and after six weeks they reckoned that they had sufficient backing to have the archbishop approach Pope Clement, to urge the Vatican's declaration of opposition and censure.

This duly followed, and was sufficiently effective to modify greatly the Spaniards' behaviour, this aided by the Portuguese fleet being powerful and jealous of the Spanish efforts to control the seas, even though King Philip the Second had now become King of Portugal also.

Thomas's part in the endeavour recommended him to still wider admiration.

All this, by the spring of 1602, had made Thomas's name

widely renowned in Scotland, as well as on the Continent. King James was appreciative, with George Heriot lending him more money to increase his private involvement in the East India Company. James, learning of Thomas's return to Edinburgh, summoned him before the royal presence at Holyrood.

"Man, Hope," he was greeted, "I'm aye hearing o' your doings and ploys. You're the right active yin. I could dae wi' ithers the likes o' you. This o' the East India Company: it pays gey weel. I could dae wi' mair o' it, tae. Geordie Heriot says it's worth paying moneys intae – and he's richt wise on the like. He's daeing sae himsel'. *You* ken aboot it a'. Is it like to stay o' profit, or no'? Or even to get better? Thae accursed Spaniards – are they like to damage it?"

"I judge that they are being contained, Sire. All are uniting against them, even the Portuguese. And *they* have the ships. So the prospects are good for the company."

"That's what Heriot says. Sae – you tae! He lends me money, you ken. Ooh, aye, at the interest, mind. But nae sae hard on me, his liege-lord, as on ithers, he says. This o' the spice trade wi' the Indies, if it's like to better, there's gain to be had there. You're the yin to ken. What say you, man?"

"I agree, Your Grace. The company, with its Dutch monopoly, is in a position greatly to expand, keep on growing, getting larger, richer."

"*You* hae moneys in it?"

"A little, Sire. But I am not a rich man. I would have more in it, if I could."

"Is it worth me borrowing mair from Heriot?"

"I would say so, Sire. He himself is seeking more. But winning more shares is not so easy. Those who hold them know what is good for them, and hold on to them."

"The company, as it grows, will issue mair, belike. *You*, I'm tell't, are close tae thae Dutchmen whae run it. If you would hae mair – then sae would I. Can you see tae it, man? For me?"

"If Your Grace so wishes."

"Aye. The three o' us. Geordie Heriot, yoursel' and me. Hoo say you?"

"I would do what I could, Sire."

"Guid! Guid! See you, my mither wasna wise in this o' gold and siller. As in much else, forbye! A bonnie, fine woman, but no' canny wi' her purse-strings. She left me wi' the royal coffers empty. Sae, I need to fill them. Aid me in this o' the India Company, and I'll thank you. Will you?"

"I will, Sire."

"I'ph'mmm. See you, would a bit lift in the style o' you aid you in this? Gie you mair muscle in it?"

"How mean you, Sire?"

"I mean that *I* can gie you that. I can mak knights! As ithers canna dae. If you were *Sir* Thomas Hope, would that gie you mair o' the muscle?"

Thomas blinked. "I . . . I do not know, Your Grace. I have never thought of the like. I am but a merchant-burgess's son . . ."

"Och, there's merchants got themsel's knighted afore this! How say you?"

Thomas wagged his head, at a loss for words.

"It would dae you nae herm, man. Gie you a bit mair standing, wi' thae Dutchmen and the likes, no? And show that you've gotten *me* behind you. Aye, and teach yon dreich uncle o' yourn, Edward Hope, to mind his wheesht!"

Thomas had forgotten that the king knew his Uncle Edward. "I am scarce worthy, Sire . . ."

"I'll be the judge o' that. See you, awa' ben to thae fowk in the bit hall here. Fetch you the Earl o' Moray, wi' his sword. He's my kinsman – in bystartry, mind. And we'll see tae this."

It was a royal command. Thomas did as he was ordered. In the noisy hall of the abbey, full of drinking courtiers and nobles, he had some difficulty in picking out James Stewart, Earl of Moray, and informing him that the King's Grace required his presence in the anteroom. And with a sword.

Moray stared. "A sword! What is this? My royal nephew much dislikes cold steel. What's to do?"

"That is not for me to say, my lord. But he would so have it."

Shrugging, the earl accompanied him back to the anteroom, with an attendant's sword.

"Aye, James," the monarch greeted them. "Here's work for your sword. *You* hud it, and I'll put my hand on it. Will gie this Hope a bit tap wi' it. Kneel you, man Thomas. Aye, just here."

Doing as he was told, Thomas knelt there on the anteroom floor, while Moray held out the sword and the king rather gingerly put a couple of fingers on the hilt, leaving the earl to do any wielding.

Down on one shoulder, then on the other, the blade fell, quite heavily.

"Thomas Hope, herewith I dub thee knight, man. Thus, and thus. Be thou guid knight until thy life's end, see you. Aye. Arise, Sir Thomas!"

He got to his feet, all but shaking his head at how brief and simple a rite it was to change a man's status from simple citizen to one of titled notable designation. He bowed, wordless, as the king turned away.

"That's that, then," James said. "You'll see to my shares

47

in yon company, mind. And keep me advisit as tae what's what. You, and Geordie Heriot."

"I shall, Sire. And, and I thank you!"

"Weel you may! See you repay me. Off wi' you."

Thomas backed out of the presence, a knight.

It took a while for the realisation of his new style and rank to sink in, he having to remind himself of it now and again. What would Harry have to say to this? But Harry was afar off, in Antwerp. His three uncles offered no congratulations, possibly deeming him unworthy and upjumped. It was not until he paid another visit to Wallyford House that he gained any acknowledgment.

"Ha, Sir Thomas!" John Bennett greeted him. "Salutations! Your many achievements rewarded, after a fashion. Here is recognition, well deserved. King Jamie may be the Wisest Fool in Christendom, but this time he has shown good sense."

"Is that it? Or merely to have me prove useful to him, hereafter?"

"Do not sound so humble," Elizabeth said, as her father left them to attend to his affairs. "He clearly sees you as one to be watched and favoured. As may others."

"Even yourself, perhaps? A little!"

"Who knows? *My* favours would be . . . otherwise!"

"I would hope so! No harm in hoping?"

"Does knighthood entitle you to more than being called 'sir'?"

"I would not claim so. But . . ." He left the rest unsaid.

That young woman was proficient in raising her eyebrows significantly. "Is it still warm enough for a swim, think you?"

"Why, yes. And you would warm up any man's day!"

"Is that being knightly? Or just . . . kind?"

"The kindness would be on your part. In accepting my company."

"Well, I did not suffer for it the last time!"

"How do I answer that? I make no promises."

"To do, or not to do – what?"

"To be . . . constrained. Diffident."

"Are you capable of that?"

"Would you go swimming with me if you thought me not? I was so, last time."

"And you *needed* to be so?"

"Yes, indeed. You are such as to tempt a man to be otherwise! In your looks and person, lass."

"Oh. So it is inadvisable to repeat the behaviour?"

"I must just seek to restrain myself, I suppose."

"And I must not too greatly impose on your abilities in that respect? Perhaps then we ought not to go swimming? Or, you on one side of the pool, I on the other?"

"We might meet in the middle. Or I could swim across."

"So you could. Dear me, the problems!"

"Can you accept my knightly promise to behave myself?"

"Are you knights so disciplined?"

"I am but newly knighted. So . . . !"

Smiling, she led the way to their horses.

They spurred on to the Gledsmuir and the lochan.

As before, Elizabeth went behind her bush to undress, Thomas wondering why this womanly modesty, when she was going to appear thereafter totally unclad. He himself flung off his clothes heedless, and was into the pool splashing, to welcome her with flicks of water.

"You are beauteous!" he exclaimed. "All of you!"

"Flattery will get you nowhere, sir!"

"I am well content with where I am!"

"Ah! Unambitious?"

"I would not say that."

They swam around, side by side.

Presently Elizabeth led the way out, and they commenced the running-and-drying process, she holding her breasts more or less steady.

"I would that I could do that for you!" he declared. "But . . ."

"*You* are not so . . . burdened! Except . . . !" She gave a little laugh.

"The sight of you, er, moves me!"

"So I see. We both have our bodily . . . appendages."

"Yours are a notable gift to the eyes. Mine, less so!"

"Who are *you* to know what female eyes esteem? Unless you have been informed, ere this?"

Back at their clothes, when Elizabeth would have gone on to her bush, Thomas took her arm to press her to sit. She did not shake him off, and he seated himself beside her on the grass, and close, close enough for his arm to encircle her waist, this without it being pushed away.

"This is . . . good!" he declared.

"You have said that before, if I mind aright."

"That does not make it the less so. And . . . appreciated. In present company."

"Yes. The company makes a difference."

"You do not object to *my* company?"

"Would I be sitting here, naked, if I did?"

His hand all but involuntarily moved up from her waist to under the swelling of her bosom. "You are very lovely. And kind."

"Kind? What of kindness? Does it not imply some sacrifice? I am not aware of such, in this."

"Yet you *are* kind. And towards myself. And without any reason to be so."

"No? A quite famous man. And myself the daughter of a small laird."

"The size of your father's lairdship has nothing to do with it. It is *you* that I want."

"Want?"

"Aye, want. Yourself. All of you. Not just . . . this." His hand moved up further to cup her breast, finger and thumb fondling the nipple. "I want you, all of you, need you. For myself. Just you, Elizabeth. Not to be thus kind to me. But to be mine. Mine only." He covered his groin with his other arm. "Dare I hope?"

"I cannot stop you hoping, Thomas."

"Would you wish to?"

"No-o-o. Not if you mean yours and only yours. For all time, hereafter. And you *mine*, no other's, no other woman's. I will not share you with another. Beyond . . . this."

Almost roughly he jerked her round, to face him, searching her eyes. "I love and adore you, Elizabeth!" he exclaimed. "I do! I do! Love! Need! Desire! Will . . . will you have me?"

She did not answer, save with her lips, her wordless open lips.

They kissed and kissed, he more vehemently, passionately, searchingly, than he knew, all but devouring her. Not that she complained.

There was no need for more words for a while. But when the male hands began to stray downwards, she gently pushed them up again to her breasts.

"Patience, dear Thomas," she got out. "Let us be patient. Especially unclad as we are! We could . . . spoil it. This, these moments of bliss. Which we have discovered. We have learned that we love one another. This no . . . no idle fancy. So – so we must cherish this new-found knowledge. The joy of it. Not go over-fast , . ."

"I have known it for long. Or what seems long! And now . . . !"

"Yes, now it is out. Our love. For I too have known it in my heart. Let us have joy, yes – but keep our heads as well as our hearts. And bodies! That will come . . ."

"I suppose so. If you wish it. Perhaps you are right. But . . . !"

"Naked as we are – yes, I ask it of you, my dear. For our better joy hereafter."

"If you say so. But you are temptation to any man, temptation personified to me."

"Poor Thomas!"

"Your father? He will agree to have me marry you? Has not got other plans?"

"Oh, I think that he will, yes. The way he has looked at the pair of us! He has not warned me against you!"

"When? When may we wed?"

"Dear me, give me a little time, impatient one. A woman has much to consider before she marries, see you. But not long, I promise you."

"I have no landed property to make you lady over. You will be Lady Hope only in name. But I will seek one – an estate. As good as I can afford. Where, think you? Where would you wish to make your, *our*, new home?"

"Sakes, Thomas – you go so fast! I have not got the length of thinking of the like. Give me time!"

"I want you! So soon as possible, lass. And I must have a house to take you to. Your father will demand that. Todd's Close, in Edinburgh's High Street, is no place for a bride. I can afford some small estate, with Geordie Heriot's assistance. Sell him some of my company shares. We Hopes have not been lairds. But I would have you to settle where you would wish to be."

"Well . . . somewhere in Fife, perhaps? My mother came from near Ceres, in Fife. I have always liked those parts. *Her* father was a small laird at Callange. Somewhere thereabouts would be pleasing. But – no need to go buying land, Thomas my love. It is *you* I would have, not earth and property."

"Your father may think otherwise. Besides, it would be *my* wish also, to take you to where you could be Lady Hope. The least I could do. Think on it. I have to go to the Low Countries on matters of the company and the spice and diamond trade. Ah! This of diamonds. I have one. I have had one this while. Given me by the bargomaster and magistrates of Amsterdam. Now I will have a use for it. A fine piece. My wedding gift to you! I will bring it back from Antwerp. Harry, my brother, holds it for me."

"Gracious me! A diamond! What would I do with the like?"

"Wear it. I will have it mounted on a gold chain. Show that, although you are wedding no landed laird, you wed no pauper either!"

"What am I getting myself into? Having to play the diamond-wearing Lady Hope!"

"You will survive it. And adorn the diamond! If *I* will survive, waiting until we are wed! When?"

"How long will you be gone to the Low Countries?"

"No longer than I can help, believe me. Say three weeks, ships allowing."

"That will probably be enough . . ."

"More than enough! For me." His hands were busy again, and had to be slapped back. "You will have it all arranged while I am away? Your father agreeing. At Tranent kirk, no doubt, your minister there marrying us. I will bring my brother back with me, if it is possible, to act my groomsman. Three weeks, without seeing you! What a thought!"

"Are bridegrooms always so eager? After all, here you are, holding me naked in your arms. You have that already!"

"I want more, much more."

"Greedy! And perhaps you will find a Dutch lady to make do with, as you wait?"

"Would you have me to do that?"

"I would prefer not, no. You men!" She stirred in his arms. "Come, one more swim. Then off with us."

Reluctantly he released her.

"You will find a ship at Leith?"

"There should be little problem. There is much trading with the Netherlands, especially in Lammermuir wool and fleeces. And if not direct to Amsterdam, then to Dieppe, from where there is constant coming and going. I have to see George Heriot first."

Some more bathing, a little more kissing and fondling, and it was back to Wallyford, and the parting. Three weeks . . .

6

At Antwerp, Harry put his brother into the picture as to what was going on, especially with the East India Company. He, Harry, was prospering, notably so; indeed he was becoming considerably more wealthy than Thomas, who found himself being offered a loan, and on easier terms than might be had from George Heriot, to help to buy a property in Fife. Borrowing, even from his brother, was not Thomas's aim, however. He was for selling some of his East Indies shares – and knew where to go to get the best prices.

He was not unsuccessful in this, for the company was ever expanding, the Spanish threat being countered, so shares were moving upwards, a sound investment, even in the short term. Harry's contacts were useful, encouraging.

His diamond was collected, and presented to a jewellery craftsman to be set in gold and hung on a chain.

His brother was much impressed with Thomas's attainment of knighthood. He declared that this would prove useful, here in the Low Countries, titles being esteemed.

Thomas had King James's interests to see to, as well as his own, and his evident links with the monarch did his credit no harm. Harry could use this to his own advantage also, even the East India Company not deprecating expressed royal concern.

After a busy ten days in the Low Countries, Thomas found a vessel to take him back to Leith, his finances in good order.

It was a joy to get back to Elizabeth, who proved to have been almost as busy as had he. All was prepared for the wedding at Tranent, bridal attendants arranged, a celebration meal at Wallyford House, even gypsy musicians and entertainers to enhance the occasion.

But first there was this important matter of landed property to see to, for the guests must be informed that the groom, as well as being a knight, had lairdly status. An interview with King James, at Stirling, this over his East Indies shares, provided the necessary authority. To help to purchase these extra shares, the monarch would sell Thomas an appendage portion at the extreme eastern end of the royal hunting-forest of Falkland, in Fife – these the lands of Craighall in the parish of Ceres, in Stratheden, if he so desired. How much ground he would be prepared to buy was for him to decide.

So a visit over to Fife was called for. And since Elizabeth and Thomas were now betrothed, her father agreed that they could go off together to view the terrain.

It was only a dozen or so miles across the Firth of Forth to the Fife shore at Largo; whereas to ride thither, round-about, by Stirling, would be almost one hundred miles. So a crossing in a fishing-boat was the answer, and to hire horses thereafter.

They had no difficulty in finding a fishing-boat at Cockenzie to take them across the estuary on its way out into the Norse Sea; and at Largo garrons were available. From there, Ceres lay almost due north some seven miles, with this Craighall a mile nearer.

So side by side they rode up the Boghall Burn, past Pitcruivie Castle of the Lindsays, then Balcormo, to circle the modest height of Norrie's Law, and on past Bandirran to reach the Craighall burn, with Craighall itself a half-mile further. Approaching it they had to pass a deep wooded den of the burn, which pleased Elizabeth with its dramatic ravine and rushing waters.

Craighall proved to be only a farm, with a water-mill, although the name had seemed to indicate some more lofty dwelling. Admittedly there were the green ramparts of an ancient Pictish fort on a prominence, but such remains could not be termed a hall. Thomas suggested that the name might be but a corruption of craig, meaning height, and haugh, a burn's meadowland below.

Whatever the meaning behind the name, the area was attractive scenically, and both were happy to have it as the site of their home-to-be. Thomas would have a tower-house built on a spur of hillock. This of course would take time, so, after the wedding, they would have to dwell partly at Todd's Close and partly at Wallyford.

King James expedited the transfer of the land to Thomas, so that he could call himself Hope of Craighall at the wedding, and indicated his satisfaction with the new laird by creating the property a barony, with the privileges that went with that style, these including a seat in the Scottish parliament.

The visit of inspection took them most of the day, and they could not get back across Forth that evening, so it meant spending the night somewhere there in Fife. This had not failed to occur to Thomas, and he wondered how Elizabeth would consider it. If she had done so already, she did not seem concerned. She declared that they would surely find a suitable place at Ceres.

There were indeed three or four inns at the little market-town. Choosing the best-seeming, they sought accommodation. A man and a woman arriving together were to be looked upon as husband and wife; and they were conducted up to a chamber with a large double bed, there appearing to be no others vacant. Glancing at Elizabeth, Thomas cleared his throat, but waving a hand at him, she announced that this would serve them, and ordered their gear to be brought up from the horses.

"You . . . you do not object? To us sharing? Sharing a room for the night?" he asked. "If so, I can go to one of the other inns."

"Why do that?" she enquired. "We shall soon be sharing our nights together, all or most of them. It is a large bed, I see. And we can remain well apart. That woman called it an apartment. We can make it that! If I can trust you not to . . . encroach?"

"I . . . I think that you can. If so *you* are prepared?"

"If I was not – think you that I would be marrying you? We have been together naked, sufficiently often, without misbehaving. This will be none so difficult."

He wondered at that, but did not say so.

When it came to retiring time and they climbed to that room, there was the usual tub of warm water, for washing themselves, steaming there. Elizabeth nodded approval, and promptly began to discard her clothing.

"I will bathe first, and you can wash my back, if you will," she said, entirely practical about it.

He had never actually done the like, and in the circumstances made quite a performance of it, not restricting himself to her back. She shook her head over this, but allowed him to satisfy himself fairly fully, until his physical arousal had her checking him.

"Sufficient, sir!" she ordered. "Do not make our apart-keeping the more difficult for you. Even for myself, perhaps. We must behave patiently, no? That one day, or night, and soon, we can do otherwise!"

"You can be somewhat cruel, woman!"

"Only to be kinder hereafter."

She played her part in the back-washing rather less sedulously, and was reaching for the towel to dry herself when Thomas insisted on performing this service also.

"I appear to be acquiring a zealot for cleanliness," she observed. "Is that part of knight-errantry?"

"I would not leave a task half done!"

"You choose your tasks with some calculation! Enough! Now, now for the shared bed. And more tasks over our different parts of it."

He pursed lips rather than made promises.

She got under the blankets first, keeping well to one side. He did not exactly follow suit, positioning himself towards the middle. And promptly a hand reached out to her.

She firmly took it, and returned it to him. "I thought that we had agreed to this of some, some apartment?" she reminded. "See you, it is no cold night. Shall we roll up one of these blankets and place it between us? As an aid?"

"No – no need. That will not be necessary. Only – let me touch you on occasion, lass. Just a touch, a little stroking. You do not realise just how tempting you are. In your person, as in all else."

"I offer you this blanket between."

"Have it so, then. But I would reach over it, now and then. To remind you that I am there! And *with*holding myself from holding you."

"Are we not going to bed to sleep, not to be restraining ourselves? I have told you, the night will come when we need not. But not yet. If it is going to be so great a travail for you, why not take that blanket and sleep on the floor? Or shall I?"

"God forbid! No, we shall manage it, woman! Somehow. But a touch, on occasion?"

"Very well. Is it unfortunate that this inn had only the one chamber for us? Over-great a trial for you?"

"Perhaps. But – no! This is still better than having two rooms. For me, at least. Oh, Elizabeth – this waiting! Waiting until we can be as one together! You and me."

"None so long now, dear man. You will, I judge, thank me one day. Now, roll up this blanket . . ."

So they bedded down together. It was only moments before his hand came over the roll of blanket to touch her. She took it in one of her own, and held it against her side, where it rose and fell with her deep breathing.

She was kind. But not over-kind. And she slept before he did, that night.

They had two days of riding around Fife, and two nights of sleeping together, this with restraint but undeniable pleasure nevertheless, Thomas reluctantly accepting that this was right as well as proper.

On learning that King James was again at Falkland, hunting, they rode thither. Thomas joined in a chase, Elizabeth preferring to remain with Queen Anne and little Prince Charles, now nearly two years old, this partly to escape the attentions of the courtier, Patrick, Master of Gray, who had a marked appreciation of good-looking women, and made no attempts to conceal it.

Thomas was never to forget that first hunt with the monarch – for there were others later – because, when they had managed to corner and slay a stag, nothing would do but that James had one of the others to slit open the creature's belly with his dirk, this of cold steel ever the king's antipathy, to reveal its steaming entrails; whereupon the royal boots were removed, and the king stepped into the pile of guts to paddle his feet therein, because he believed that such was good for rheumatism, from which he suffered. There was no washing of feet thereafter before the boots were re-donned, water in James's opinion being of little necessity, within the human frame or without. What Anne of Denmark thought of this, when she had to share a bed with her husband, was not reported. The monarch tended to be odd in bed otherwise also, not only in that he insisted on wearing a hat at night, and this no mere sleeping-cap, because, when he was young, at Stirling Castle, a bat had somehow got itself into the rather tattered canopy of the great bed and deposited some of its droppings on James's head. Small wonder that Anne was known to prefer her own room in palaces and castles. Not that her isolation worried the king, who was not greatly interested in womenfolk anyway.

After this hunt he had a word with Thomas, seeking news of the East India Company and share prices, and also wondering whether English law differed from Scots in any marked degree? For, he confided, Elizabeth Tudor's health was deteriorating rapidly, and it looked as though he would be finding himself king of her England before long. It would be useful for him to know how the laws differed.

Thomas admitted that he was not expert on English law, being more knowledgeable on French and Dutch. But he would discover the basics of it.

"Aye, dae that. I'ph'mm. I'm tell't you're intending to wed yon lassie Bennett, Wallyford's dochter. Could you no' dae better than that, man? She's bonnie enough, aye; but in your position you could belike wed some lord's dochter, and gain some lands wi' it."

"I am very well pleased with Elizabeth, Sire – just

thankful that she will have me. We shall be content with Craighall and its barony."

"Sae you're no' ambitious, Hope man? Maist are, I've found. And seek *my* aid in it. No' you? Geordie Heriot's no' either. I've offered him a knighthood, even a baronetcy, but he doesna want it."

"There are ambitions and ambitions, Sire, are there not? Heriot's must be otherwise. Mine is to live a quietly rewarding life, with Elizabeth Bennett, hopefully have a family, make a good home at this Craighall, serve Your Grace well – and, to be sure, look forward, if I may, to a still more worthy destiny hereafter. Is that a fair and honest ambition?"

"Man, yon's no' bad, no' bad at a'. For a lawyer! I'll mind it . . ."

The marriage was celebrated in Tranent kirk, after some agitation on Thomas's part by the delayed arrival of brother Harry to act groomsman, a storm at sea responsible and his ship having to shelter at Newcastle. The couple sought a simple ceremony and no great feasting and revelry afterwards, which suited John Bennett, a man averse to display.

So, after being duly declared man and wife, a fairly moderate celebration followed, at which Thomas presented his bride with the great diamond on its gold chain, hanging it round her neck ceremoniously, to applause. Then the pair were seen off with much of pleasantries and good advice, to ride for Edinburgh and Todd's Close, no notable establishment for a marriage night, but it was too late in the day to seek more distant lodging – and it was considered unsuitable to remain at Wallyford House.

Actually, it was Thomas's plan to combine business with

pleasure, and take his bride to see Antwerp and Amsterdam and thereabouts. Harry, coming to Edinburgh for the wedding, was going back in his own vessel from Leith the next day; so they would sail with him, and some nights were to be passed aboard ship. Fortunately Elizabeth was a good sailor, and there were no complaints.

Meantime, they retired fairly early that night, at Todd's Close, the bride shaking her head over the domestic arrangements there and declaring that her husband had much to learn about housekeeping. He countered by suggesting that *she* had something to learn that night! As, for that matter, had he, whatever their previous experiences together.

There was, to be sure, nothing new about disrobing and washing each other, even sharing a bed – this one much less large than that they had occupied before. But after that it would be new territory.

"Are you still the eager male?" she asked, as he climbed in beside her. "If so, have some mercy, I pray you. I am less knowledgeable, perhaps. So, bear with me, if you can!"

"What makes you think that I am so well informed in this?"

"You men do not reach manhood without some learning, I judge?"

"Do not you, from talk if nothing else?"

"Talk is scarcely enough preparation."

"You are not dreading this, my love?"

"No. Not that. Only, shall we say a little anxious. Anxious that I, that *we*, come together . . . kindly. That I do not disappoint. That our wedding night is all that you hope for."

"And you. We are very much together in this. In more ways than one. See you, I am going to kiss you. All over."

"That will scarcely be new for you."

"It will, in some degree. As you will discover!"

"Mmm."

He started with her hair, her brow, her ears, her lips, her neck, her shoulders, her breasts, lingering over these. Then on, she running her fingers through his head of hair. He sought not to hurry his attentions, restraining himself, kissing, kissing. And was rewarded by her reactions, gradual at first, then growing, stirring, responding, this in her person as well as her voice.

Joyfully they were one, as they had longed to be. One, then and for always. Fulfilled.

7

Next day it was for Leith and Harry's ship. But before sailing, Thomas sought out a master-mason recommended to him, and presented him with a rough map that he had drawn of the Craighall area, ordering a tower-house to be built, and pointing out what he judged to be the most suitable site. No great fortalice was asked for, but a fairly simple L-planned building of four storeys and a garret, this last within a parapet-walk with angle turrets corbelled out to project at the five outer corners, and a circular stair tower in the angle, the doorway at its foot. Internally, the kitchen, great fireplace and oven were in the stone-vaulted basement, a hall on the first floor, with anteroom, and bed-chambers above. The mason had constructed the like before, and knew what was required. Thomas left a deposit of moneys with him.

Then it was aboard ship for Sir Thomas and Lady Hope, Elizabeth declaring that she would search out some worthy furnishings and wall-hangings to bring back with them from the Low Countries.

So the second night of marriage was spent in a ship's cabin, with single bunks set one above another. So the love-making, after a little experimenting on the lower one, it was decided should be on blankets spread on the floor. And when they had satisfied themselves thus, and having to adjust as the ship rolled in the Norse Sea swells, there was debate as to which of them should occupy the lower and which the upper bed. Elizabeth decided that, with the vessel's tossing, the upper sleeper might well be flung out, so she would allow her husband that privilege.

Thomas passed a somewhat wakeful night, finding himself having to clutch the edge of his shelf to prevent himself on occasion from the fate feared. Elizabeth seemed to sleep soundly.

Oddly, once the ship was out of the Firth of Forth, the seas seemed to moderate, and instead of pitching and tossing they rolled rather, as they headed southwards. They made good time of it, for the wind, although strong, was from the north-east, and it filled their sails effectively. But it made chilly voyaging.

In three days and nights they reached Amsterdam. Elizabeth was fascinated by what she saw there, the innumerable canals, the many bridges over them, some of these actually bearing houses, the tall gabled and brightly painted tenements, the great churches and shrines, and the busy market-places with traders selling their wares, especially their great variety of cheeses. She kept seeing desirable items that she had to be restrained from buying, to Thomas's head-shakings, although wealthy Harry did humour her in this. It might be the diamond capital of Europe, and the base of the East India Company, from which came most of Thomas's income, but she was ruefully told that she must be content with what she already had. If it was worldly goods and adornments she sought, she ought to have married Harry, not his brother.

On to Antwerp, which much impressed her, with its miles of docks, shipyards, mills and factories, but more with its academies of various sciences and skills, its halls hung with paintings by Titian, Massys, Bruegel, Dürer, Memling, Weyden and others, the great six-aisled cathedral with its lofty spire, its one hundred and twenty-five pillars and carillon of ninety-nine bells which rang out over the entire city, its handsome Exchange, claimed to be the finest commercial building in the world. She perceived why Harry chose to make Antwerp his base.

At the Exchange, Thomas was able to purchase more company shares, some few for himself but more for George Heriot and King James – how many were in the nature of a loan from the banker to the monarch he was uncertain – this really the object of the visit, the price ever rising as the trade increased, and making his own modest holding the more valuable. Was it worth borrowing more to invest? Jinglin' Geordie clearly thought it was, and he should know. Their Edinburgh seemed a very inconsiderable capital compared with Antwerp and Amsterdam, however much more dramatic in its appearance and scenery.

Thomas all but emptied his never overfull purse at the Exchange, to purchase a few more shares for himself, Elizabeth doubtful, especially as he was urging her to be frugal and sparing in her spending. Had they not their new home which they were having built at Craighall to furnish and make pleasing and comfortable?

Male and female priorities somewhat clashed.

In the circumstances, Thomas was all but relieved when, his own business done, Harry announced it advisable not to delay their return to Scotland. The rumour was that Queen Elizabeth Tudor was on her death-bed, and her demise would undoubtedly mean major changes for Scotland as well as her England.

At Leith they learned that Elizabeth had indeed died, three days before, on 24 March, and the two kingdoms were in a state of excitement and questioning. But at least there seemed to be no doubt as to the English succession, for with all but her last breath the queen had named James as her heir, this rejecting the claims of the Lady Arabella Stewart, her other cousin and also cousin of James. Arabella was the niece of Darnley, Mary, Queen of Scots' husband and James's father, so this put her close to both thrones.

James Stewart was now to add the throne of England to that of Scotland, something that had been the driving ambition of the southern monarchy for centuries. What would this result in? England had ten times the population of the northern kingdom, and was infinitely the more wealthy and important in world affairs, even though Scotland had been a kingdom hundreds of years before England's various divisions and territories united to become a nation. Would the larger, richer realm be prepared to be ruled from the lesser northern one? It seemed highly unlikely. And would James Stewart remain in Scotland now? And what of Wales and Ireland? All four nations seethed with questions.

Knowing James, and his preoccupation with money and what it could do, Thomas had little doubt. The king would head southwards with scant delay, and London become his seat and capital instead of Edinburgh and Stirling. Great change would come to Scotland, inevitably.

It was not long before Thomas was sent for from Stirling, just as Elizabeth and he were about to set off for Fife, to discover how the building at Craighall was progressing. They could not yet make the long ride up the south side of Forth, and thereafter along the north coast, thirty-five miles and then another fifty.

King James was in a state of great excitement, slobbering wetly as he talked. He now had his far-out cousin, Ludovick, Duke of Lennox, with him. He was for London at the soonest, and wanted Thomas to accompany him, he being so knowledgeable as to money matters and the law.

"Thae English lords will be seeking to use and bumbaze me, Hope man," he declared. "Vicky here's right guid, but he doesna ken the law and a' this o' moneys and shares and the like. And Tam o' the Coogate maun bide here. Sae you've to go wi' me, see you. No' to bide there, necessar, but to help me wi' thae English lords and lawmen. They can be right proud and lofty. Yon Cecil, or Burleigh as they ca' him noo, in especial. You'll gie me a hand."

"But I am newly married, Sire! And we are seeking to make a new home, over in Fife. Which your Grace has made into a barony . . ."

"Och, you can bring the lassie wi' you. She'll like it fine. Aye – and this o' the barony. It gies you a seat in the parliament, mind. I've called one. And nae forty days' notice this time. I canna hae that, when I'm to mak for London, wi' nae delay. Aye, attend you it. It's here, at Stirling, in eight days' time. And then I'm for London, and you."

"As you command, Sire . . ."

So Thomas attended his first parliament as laird. He was much interested in the proceedings, Elizabeth watching all from a gallery of the Great Hall of Stirling Castle.

The king was led in by the Lord Lyon King of Arms, all standing to receive him as he shambled over to sit on the throne-like chair. He did not conduct the business, however, that being the duty of the Chancellor, presently John, Earl of Montrose, the Graham chief. The monarch might intervene and make comments, but otherwise only preside.

Thomas sat among the barons, and there were many of them, behind the earls' benches and those of the lords of parliament, but in front of the commissioners of the shires and the provosts and representatives of the royal burghs. Since the Reformation, there were no churchmen present as such, these now having their own General Assembly.

The main business of this specially called session was, of course, the ascent of the king to the English throne, and its possible impact on Scotland. There was much concern over this, and a great number of questions to be answered. Scotland's separate identity and authority must be preserved, at all costs, and there was a danger that if the monarch and court became based in London, these might become eroded.

James, on his throne, was backed by the principal officers of state, the Earl Marischal, the Lord High Admiral, the High Justiciar, the High Constable, the Lord Chamberlain, the King-of-Arms taking his place among them as Seneschal, these standing throughout.

After an introductory prayer, the Chancellor announced the decisions made by the monarch and his Privy or Secret Council as to the government of Scotland now that His Grace would be apt to be based in London. The council would act for the monarch in the rule here, and keep in close contact with him at all times. Had this parliament any questions to raise as to these decisions by His Grace and the council?

None was forthcoming, when all this had been agreed by such trusted and reliable individuals, save for a proposal that Archibald Campbell, Earl of Argyll, should be included in the council to represent the Highland interests, this being accepted.

Thereafter the assembly moved on to more general parliamentary business, concerns and appointments.

Thomas made a contribution to the debates when he put forward a motion to the effect that Scots law should be represented permanently at the English parliament, this to ensure its authority where the interests of the two kingdoms overlapped or conflicted. This was unanimously agreed, to cheers, James nodding his head solemnly and tipping his tall hat forward in a gesture of approval.

After the adjournment, when Thomas had made his excuses, the couple set off for Craighall, late in the day as it was. They could get part-way, at least.

They halted for the night at an inn at Culross, just into Fothriff, with Elizabeth interested in Thomas's account of St Serf christening here, at his little shrine, the infant son of Thanea, daughter of King Loth of the southern Picts, who gave his name to Lothian. The child was called Kentigern but was usually known as Mungo, meaning manikin, and he later, with his mother, founded Glasgow at the junction of the Molendinar Burn with the Clyde, where its cathedral was eventually styled St Mungo's, this a story Elizabeth had not previously heard. Thomas told her also how the local laird, one Sir George Bruce, was sufficiently enterprising to have a coal-seam tapped into, which stretched out for nearly a mile beneath the waters of the firth, something hithero unknown in Scotland, with a shaft rising up for shipping the coal – this reckoned to be a wonder. The mining had been started, like so much elsewhere, by the monks, these of a Cistercian abbey closed down at the Reformation. Culross was a busy little town, producing tar, naphtha and salt as well as coal, and was all but famous for its hammermen forging girdles of iron, for the baking of scones and cakes. Nothing would do but that Elizabeth must purchase one of these before heading on, Thomas having to carry the awkward burden at his saddle-bow.

They reached Craighall by noon next day, and were glad to see considerable progress in the building of their tower-house, the walls having reached parapet level, and the corbelling, to project the angle turrets, in place. Thomas, who had consulted the Lyon King of Arms regarding a suitable escutcheon for the new knight, had decided, very much with Elizabeth's guidance, on a blue shield bearing a golden chevron or triangle, indicating the rafters of a roof over their heads, this between three bezants or gold coins bearing hunting-horns, to represent lands purchased with company money in the royal hunting area of Falkland. Surmounting this was a crest of a broken globe or world with the motto "*At Spes Infracta*", meaning "all may seem lost but hope never dies." The pair had had great discussion over its devising. Now they had to find a mason sufficiently talented to carve it in stone, to place over the tower's doorway. Their master-mason declared that there was a craftsman in St Andrews who specialised in the like.

So the work went ahead.

The interior, with its furnishings, carpeting and decoration, was now Elizabeth's concern, and she had no lack of ideas and preferences for their new home. Craighall could not be their most frequented residence, however, since Thomas's duties demanded that he must be based in Edinburgh for most of the time. So Todd's Close had to serve for that. But this little castle in Fife was to be their true retreat and home, and must reflect that standing. They had brought back much from the Continent, especially carpeting, eastern rugs, hangings and tapestries, which served as a start. But Elizabeth ranged wide to find and collect desired enhancements.

Her search was interrupted by King James's decision to leave for London without delay, this on the fifth day of April; and Thomas was commanded to attend. A great company would escort the monarch over the border to enter his new kingdom with suitable flourish.

All were to assemble outside Edinburgh's Holyrood, at nine of the clock for the first day's ride. It was fifty-seven miles, by the shortest route, to Berwick-upon-Tweed, where James intended to spend the night in the hitherto hostile castle, notorious for its obstructing of Scots, but now his, like all else. To emphasise the change, Sir Charles Percy, brother of the Earl of Northumberland, had come to escort His Majesty – as he was now to be styled instead of His Grace – to and over the border.

Thomas and Elizabeth were there, ready, like all others – except for the king himself, who had ordered the hour's start. He did not appear, and the great company waited, fidgeted and stood by their horses.

Of all informants it was no great lord or courtier who came to explain the delay, but George Heriot, the banker. James had had an argument with Queen Anne. She was not to accompany him south, he had decided, but would travel behind with the ladies at their own pace. This royal announcement created much upset among the womenfolk, for the wives of many of the lords here involved were the queen's attendants, and now they were going to be separated from their husbands. But James was adamant.

"Thae women canna ride fast enough," he told Thomas and others. "It'll tak ower lang to win tae London wi' them. They can come in their ain time. I'm no' for short bit ambulations, aye ambulations, hudden back by females."

"But, Sire!" Thomas was going to protest, but managed to restrain himself. "Many are excellent riders, my Elizabeth included," was all that he said.

"Maybe she is. But they're no' a' that way. Annie's nae sae bad, but many o' them would be a right limitation. It's

73

four hunnerd miles to London, mind. And on oor stops, we dinna want a' thae females, wi' their ploys, hindering us." James, although he rode like a sack of potatoes, as it had been described, was fond of the saddle and could cover great distances. On occasion.

Thomas had to accept the situation, like the rest of the men involved.

They rode for Berwick's castle, where the English governor was promptly dismissed and one of the king's attendants installed in his place, this resulting in a distinctly feeble repast that evening – not that this worried the monarch, who was no great eater whatever his fondness for liquor. He was never seen actually drunk, however drink-taken.

The women arrived in due course, so Thomas was able to spend the night with Elizabeth, however lacking in comfort the accommodation.

In the morning, James made a great display about crossing the bridge over Tweed into England. Led by Percy, he dismounted and went on shambling foot over the timbers, these having him shouting disapproval. They were uneven, and shook, he declared. It was a right shoogly brig, and must be replaced. He would make that his first charge on his new English treasury! He pointed at the Earl of Northumberland and the Bishop of Durham, who were there to greet him in the names of the Privy Council and Holy Church, and told them to see to it: a new and sturdy brig, now that Scotland and England were united under him.

At the far side, to the astonishment of all present, the king got down on his knees to kiss the ground, an extraordinary gesture which had the earl and bishop, like others, wondering whether they ought to be doing the same. But, in the circumstances, probably not. This was the new monarch of England greeting his additional realm's soil, strange as the gesture seemed, and none other was in that position. Embarrassed, they all stood watching.

Getting to his feet, James wagged a finger at them. "Yon was a promise, see you!" he declared. "A pledge, just. That I'll rule this land weel. Better nor Elizabeth Tudor ruled it. But she was just a woman, mind! Pair sowl!" He nodded towards Northumberland and the bishop. "You'll see! Sae – what noo?"

This was because of a diversion. Three horsemen came down from the Spittal direction and the south, a young man in travel-stained clothing and two armed attendants, drawing up at that bridge-end, close to the monarch, who shrank back, ever fearful of assault, however unlikely this might be.

The young man stared around him. "My lord of Northumberland – the king? Is the king not here?"

Many fingers pointed towards the uninspiring figure of the monarch.

Uncertainly the visitor stared, features grey with fatigue and dust. Then, leaping from the saddle, he dropped to one knee before his new and doubtful sovereign.

"Your Majesty – Sire!" he gasped, drawing something made of metal from his doublet, which had James promptly staggering back into the arms of Northumberland in alarm, taking it to be a dagger. However, it proved to be a large iron key.

"Your Majesty, most gracious and serene example of learning, humanity and piety . . ." The tired voice faded.

"Aye, man – aye?" The king, suddenly, was interested at this percipience.

The young man obviously made a great effort to rally his tired wits and recollect the rest of his prepared speech. ". . . piety, Sire. The heart's desire of all true Englishmen. Your devoted subjects, Majesty. I am John Peyton, son of the lieutenant of the Tower of London. He, my father, has sent me here hot-foot. This is the key to the said dread Tower, Sire – England's citadel. I have ridden without sleep to present it to you as you set foot on this England's devoted soil."

The Scots, including Thomas, around the monarch looked somewhat embarrassed at such magniloquent language, but James himself seemed to find nothing amiss with it. Nodding, he took the key.

"Heavy," he declared. "Right weighty. But so is yon Tower. *Parvis componere magna!* Eh, Northumberland man?"

"Er . . . no doubt, Your Majesty," the earl said blankly.

The young man was seeking to rise stiffly from his kneeling when, abruptly, the king leaned forward and pushed him back, quite roughly.

"Bide you, laddie," he was commanded. "Bide where you're at, a wee. Son o' the lieutenant, eh?" James looked round. "Vicky, you wi' your bit sword." At his kinsman's forward step, he went on. "Gie's your whinger, man." The king made it a strict rule that no one carried a sword or dirk in his royal presence; but he made an exception in the case of Duke Ludovick, the most loyal of men, whom the monarch trusted entirely, and indeed tended to look upon as a sort of bodyguard and watchdog. "Oot wi' it."

Lennox unsheathed his sword and held it out by the tip. Gingerly James took it, almost as though it were red-hot, cold steel always his anathema. He swung the weapon in a dangerous arc at the kneeling man's shoulder, only just hitting it as the other ducked hurriedly.

"Bide you still, man. I canna knight you jouking aboot." He gave another tap. "Arise, good Sir John . . . John . . .

eh, what's the laddie's name?" he demanded, peering round.

"Peyton, Sire – Peyton," Northumberland said.

"Aye, weel – arise, Sir John Peyton. Get up, man. Here, Vicky, tak it. Aye, and tak this key, forbye – it's ower heavy."

The new knight arose flushed, blinking, stammering thanks at so unexpected an honour.

James now ignored him entirely. "Now, what now? The hour's getting late."

"My castle of Norham is quite near at hand," the bishop said. "If your Majesty will honour it, this night."

"Aye, weel. So be it. The women? There's room for the women aboot the place?"

"Ample room, Sire. It is a large house. Sir Charles will see that they win to it with all these others."

"I'ph'mm. But no' *a*' the ithers. No' a' o' these are to come, see you. Some I can weel dae withoot. *Him*, for ane." And he pointed.

The monarch was indicating quite the best-looking man present, smiling, most splendidly clad, youngish: Patrick, Master of Gray, heir to the fifth Lord Gray, and since the death of the Bonnie Earl of Moray claimed by many to be the handsomest man not only in Scotland but in all Europe. Once he had been a favourite of the king, but no longer.

"You mean Gray?" Lennox asked.

"Aye. The Maister. The women dote on him – even my Annie. A scoondrel, him! The women hae nae sense, if he's got the looks!"

Patrick Gray stepped forward, and flourished a bow so deep and elaborate as to be all but a mockery. "The King's Grace, his royal self!" he exclaimed. "Your devoted and most humble servant and subject."

"D'you ca' yoursel' that, man? Betimes, I wonder!"

"Can you, Sire? Have I not always sought to attend your royal court, and show my devotion to your cause? As I shall continue to do in London."

"Na, na – you'll no', Maister! You'll bide here. See you, I'll find me plenties o' rogues in London withoot yoursel'!"

Even Patrick Gray lost his assured self-possession at that greeting, and before the company. He blinked, and bit his lip. "Your, your royal jest is . . . worthy!" he got out.

"Aye, it is that. Sae, it's fareweel to the likes o' you! Vicky o' Lennox, here, will hae to put up wi' you. Begone, Maister o' Gray!"

That man did his best, in the circumstances. He produced another excessively deep bow, with a swinging convolution of his arm to accompany it, and, turning on his heel, strolled off with every appearance of nonchalance.

James it was who glowered and looked discomfited.

Thomas, near by, tactfully sought to fill the gap. "Your Grace's court in London will have other . . . adornments!"

"Aye, nae doot! If they're the likes o' him, I'll get rid o' them tae!"

His courtiers exchanged glances.

James changed the subject. He was contemplating the new young knight, Peyton. "He'll hae to pay for his knighthood," he declared.

"Pay? For your honouring of him?" Lennox said. "Surely not."

"Aye, pay. Geordie Heriot has just tell't me that he hears the English treasury, Elizabeth's treasury, is deep in debt! D'you hear that! In debt. The woman's ill favourites hae been milking it this while. Thousands o' pounds in debt. And I've been seeking it to pay off oor *ain* Scots costs and empty coffers! It's a fair scunner! I thocht that this would be the end o' the like. Noo – this! It's damnable! But Heriot kens. Sae, moneys. This Peyton will hae to pay!" James nodded at his play on words. "Ithers likewise. This o' knighting: here's a way oot o' the mire o' debt. *I* can mak knights – ithers canna. Pay!"

"That will much reduce the honour of knighthood, Sire."

"It'll reduce the *debt*! Fowk'll pay for being knighted. A' these English lairds. Squires they ca' them – no' *esquires*, mind. Five hunnerd pounds? Or mair – a thousand! They'll pay for it."

Lennox looked at Thomas and Heriot, and shook his head, shrugging.

"Heriot, man, see tae it. A thousand pounds. Aye, and we'll mak plenties mair. Get Peyton's note-o'-hand. For a thousand pounds. He'll can pay it – his faither's lieutenant o' London Tower. And this o' ithers that I'll knight. I'll mak these English pay for their empty treasury!"

And that James did. The company grew as they pressed on into England, and so grew the knightings and the king's wealth – or at least the reduction of his indebtedness to George Heriot – for there was much hankering for knighthood. Thomas marvelled, as did others.

James Stewart would indeed bring a new dimension to the English throne.

8

Although the monarch preferred to travel without female company, Thomas Hope felt otherwise. And since James did not seem to require his attendance, he elected to ride with the ladies, as did some others, with wives and daughters. Queen Anne had quite a numerous entourage, and the men were welcomed. So Elizabeth enjoyed her husband's companionship, especially of a night, as they made their way south.

They rode comparatively slowly, large numbers of horsewomen not really concerned with haste, and no doubt fell a fair way behind the king's party. But that mattered not to Anne. There was general eagerness to welcome and offer grand hospitality to the new queen and her ever growing retinue; and these English lords and their wives had great and roomy houses compared with the stone towers and fortalices of Scotland.

Anne was clearly enjoying her journey, she at her most gracious, beaming on all, kissing children, acting a very different kind of queen from Elizabeth Tudor, who latterly had been haughty and kept her distance from lesser folk. In the fine weather, it made an agreeable progress – for a progress it became, as the company expanded the further south it went, by York and Nottingham, Leicester and Grafton, with lords and ladies joining the cavalcade, distances covered, in consequence, becoming ever shorter, whatever the king's party was achieving. By the time they reached Amersham in Buckinghamshire, Thomas and Heriot assessed that they had collected no fewer than two hundred and fifty of a cavalcade. What James would think of this addition to his assembly arriving at London and Windsor remained to be seen. Anne of Denmark perceived matters very differently from her husband, he concerned with costs, she with enjoyment.

It was at Amersham that envoys, sent by Norfolk, met the king's company to inform them that an attack of the plague had struck London, in this hot weather, and it would probably be wise to make directly for Windsor in the circumstances. James, immediately alarmed, declared that he was not going to go nearer to London than that, twenty-two miles up Thames.

So word was sent to the queen's throng to make for Windsor.

The king, much upset that he could not proceed to his English capital city given the conditions, decided to make a demonstration at Windsor by naming some knights, of a new kind to him, of the Garter, to mark his succession to the English throne, and to bind closer to him certain proud lords. He had Norfolk, as Earl Marshal, recommend suitable and useful candidates.

The two companies headed for Windsor, the token key to the Tower of London laid aside meantime.

James, and indeed all the Scots, were much impressed by Windsor's commanding size within its royal park, east of its township, an enormous stronghold founded by William the Conqueror. It apparently covered no fewer than thirteen acres, with many towers, dominated by its massive circular one on an artificial mound in the middle, this visible for miles around. One of the lesser towers was in fact called the Garter Tower. But, commanding as it was, James had to declare that it could not compare with his rock-top citadels of Edinburgh, Stirling and Dumbarton. However, it did have the accommodation required to house his two cavalcades, and even most of their attendants, the servitors being able to lodge in the town below.

The creation of the Garter knights took place next day. Thomas explained how this odd designation had come about. It seemed that, in the mid-fourteenth century, Edward the Third, during a dance of his courtiers here, had noted how one of the ladies had dropped a garter from her stocking. At the sniggering of the bystanders, the monarch rebuked them, declaring, "*Honi soit qui mal y pense*," meaning shame on him who thus thinks unsuitably. James did not fail to remark on this, with a sniff, asserting that in Scotland they did not name knights after women's underwear!

However, he did install his little son, Prince Henry of Rothesay, as the first of his Garter knightings, a gesture that brought frowns to the brows of some of the English magnates.

And it was later at this ceremony that the monarch insisted that the supporters, as they were termed, flanking the royal coat of arms, hitherto two lions rampant, should now have one of these changed into a crowned unicorn, the Scottish symbol. This caused more frowns, and mutters that there was no such animal in fact, merely Scottish myths. But it came as a royal command, and as such had to be adopted. So now the lion and the unicorn were to be on all national banners, seals, documents and illustrations.

The Earl of Nottingham, a Howard, and one of the new Garter knights, remarked to Thomas, "You, a lawyer, tell me how this came about. A laughable creature to put alongside our noble beast. A unicorn!"

"You had best ask His Grace himself," he was advised. "Our learned liege-lord might be one of the few who could tell you of it. For myself, I know only that it was shown in ancient Assyrian carvings, and the Greeks described it as an Indian wild ass with a cubit-long horn, claiming that those who were able to drink from such horn would be protected from stomach illnesses and from poison. If I mind aright, it is described in the Book of Job."

The earl looked vague as to the Book of Job.

Queen Anne remarked to Elizabeth that her husband might as well have knighted their younger son, Charles, while he was at it, since presumably it would come to that hereafter, even though he was not the heir to the throne. And she confided that another child was on the way.

Elizabeth, who was fairly sure that she herself was pregnant, did not think it suitable to return the confidence. She had now become officially one of the queen's ladies-in-waiting, on the understanding that she would only act the part when Anne was in Scotland.

The Hopes returned home thereafter, Elizabeth glad to resume the furbishing of Craighall, Thomas to superintend the planting of garden and orchard. But much legal work was awaiting him, especially concerning the Kirk's affairs, which involved much quite difficult unravelling, for the Catholic Church, although no longer the established faith of the land, still existed, and its vast properties had by no means all passed to land-hungry lords. The lawful position of some of these, their revenues from rights such as milling tithes, ancient buildings, burial-grounds and the like, were very much Thomas's concern as official Procurator and Advocate to the Church of Scotland. The disputes between the lairds of former Church lands and the Reformed parish

ministers and kirk sessions were continual and often acri-
monious and not easy to solve.

Thomas had been expecting King James to make return
visits to Scotland frequently, his homeland and where his
roots were, but this did not eventuate. And the lack of a
resident monarch, and his ability to sign documents, did
result in difficulties and delays. Ludovick of Lennox was
acting as a kind of viceroy, and a good one, but certain
matters required the king's own attention, especially in
legal decisions, and Thomas found himself having to
travel to London over-often for his choice, it not being
always possible to depute such causes to representatives.
He came to the conclusion that the journeying south and
back was much more conveniently performed by ship
than on horseback, swifter also. He came to an arrangement with the harbour-master of the port of Leith to let
him know of vessels bound for the Continent or the
Thames itself, and to have the information notified to
him, now that he was living mainly at Craighall rather
than Todd's Close, by fishermen whose boats crossed the
Forth in their netting. This proved to be a major help and
greatly eased his travel problem. Elizabeth not infre-
quently accompanied him, quite enjoying the voyaging
if the weather was kind.

That is, until she was all but ready to be brought to bed
and give birth.

A little son was forthcoming, in due course, after fairly
moderate labour, first to Thomas's anxious concern and
then to his joy. They were now a family, not just a couple,
the Hopes of Craighall.

The infant, whom they named John, or Ian, throve, and
gave them great satisfaction, however much he tended to
wake them up in the middle of the night, crying vigorously

for his mother's breast. Thomas had to get used to this, and learned to sleep through it, even though his wife did not.

This new arrival did prevent Elizabeth from accompanying her husband to London for some time, which made Thomas the more reluctant to keep making the voyage. He was, however, training up a cousin, a son of his Uncle Edward, in matters legal, and this John, a bright young man, became sufficiently able to act as representative in many matters, a great help.

In all this of legal and family preoccupations, Thomas did not omit to sail to Amsterdam and Antwerp on occasion, still the main source of his income, court fees notwithstanding. In this he was much encouraged by King James, whose East India Company shares were ever in the money-conscious monarch's mind, Thomas being his commissioner and agent in this matter. This situation gave Thomas fairly frequent access to his liege-lord, which had its advantages, although sometimes it could have unwanted complications, James being the man he was.

On one of his visits to London, reporting on the East India Company shares position, the monarch loaded a different task on him.

"Thae isles ca'd the Faroes," he said. "You ken them?"

"I know *of* them, Sire. But I have never visited them."

"Aye, weel. My Annie says they belong to Denmark. If that's so, I could mebbe buy them, for her brother, yon's Christian the Fourth, the king there, is right hard put to it for moneys, and Annie says that he would sell. Thae Faroes are nane sae far north o' Orkney and the Shetlands. And if they were a pairt o' Scotland I could win the market for ivory. It's like Iceland, I'm tell't, a great place for thae walrus-beasts, wi' the ivory tusks. Ivory's right precious. Andrew Wood, the admiral – d'you mind o' him? He gathered tusks yonder, to sell to thae Hansa merchants. I could hae the same done. I'm no' right sure whether thae isles belong to Norway or Denmark. Mind, the twa are baith under the rule o' Annie's brother, Christian, sae it doesna right matter. You're right clever in siclike matters, Hope man. Find oot for me. And if it's Denmark, Christian'll sell, she says. But if it's Norway, she's no sae sure – his Norway throne's different, someways. He doesna seem to care aboot the ivory. But *I* dae! Geordie Heriot'll loan me the moneys to buy thae isles frae Christian."

"I will discover what I can, Your Grace. Norway is much nearer, I'd say, than Denmark to the Faroes."

"Find you oot, then. You aye find ships to take you to Amsterdam and the like. Get yin to tak you north, instead. Dae that."

"If so you command, Sire." That sounded scarcely enthusiastic.

"I dae, man."

So, however reluctantly, Thomas was faced with a northerly voyage. It occurred to him that he could take Elizabeth and little Ianie, as they were calling him, and make something of a holiday of it.

His enquiries proved that the Faroes belonged to Denmark, not Norway, which would make it possible for King Christian to sell – if he would.

Finding a ship to take them to the Faroes was none so easy, the isles not being of concern to Scots merchants. He was advised that he should sail from Leith to Shetland, and there find a fishing-boat to take him the two hundred further miles north-westwards, Shetlanders apparently much favouring the Faroes Bank shallows for fishing. It seemed a long journey for fishing-boats, but he was assured that the Shetland ones tended to be large enough. Could he risk taking Elizabeth and the child on such a voyage? She assured that he could.

There was no difficulty in getting a vessel going to the Shetlands from Leith, this an easy sail once they had negotiated the Orkney roosts, as they were called, tidal whirlpools around those islands caused by submarine mountains in the Pentland Firth, a heaving and tossing experience. At Lerwick, the main town and port of Shetland, they saw that there were many larger fishing-boats moored there than they were apt to see elsewhere; and enquiries elicited that not a few of these worked the Faroes Bank, a vast area of shallows abounding in cod and halibut.

They had to wait three days for one of these to take them, and with accommodation modest to say the least for a woman and child. But Elizabeth was quite prepared to put up with this.

They set sail, on quite a lengthy voyage north by west. The weather was fair, and not unpleasant, except for occasional showers of very cold rain, all but sleet. But when they neared the Faroes, halfway to Iceland, they encountered different conditions, the roosts hereabouts being stronger than those of Orkney waters, and storms more frequent. If King James wanted the Faroes for Scotland, then the ivory tusks would have to be valuable indeed.

They found these isles numerous; over a score of them, great and small, they counted, and seemingly many of them inhabited. Between them the currents were fierce. Their cliffs were enormous, loftily impressive, reaching well over one thousand feet, with great waves sending up clouds of spray at their bases. There were mountains, steep but with strangely flat summits, which presumably meant that they had once formed a high plateau until the ice carved them up. Reaching into the larger isles were deep and narrow fjords, from which fishing-boats issued on occasion, so these must provide sheltered havens and villages; their skipper claimed that there was quite a large population, of possibly fifteen thousand, descendants of the Vikings, like that of Iceland. There appeared to be no trees, however, which must be a great handicap, especially for boat-building, timber presumably having to be imported from Norway. Peat must be the fuel for the fires. They could see smoke rising from the houses and blown all but horizontally in the prevailing northerly wind.

Their vessel drew into the capital, if so it could be styled, named Tórshavn, this on the isle of Streymoy, behind which reared a high mountain, similar to such in the Scots Hebrides. Here Thomas made his enquiries.

Thomas gained the impression that his liege-lord should be advised not to seek to purchase these islands from Queen Anne's brother. There appeared to be no real advantage for Scotland in owning them. This of walrus tusks was surely insufficient as compensation. Asking about the ivory, he found his Tórshavn informants uninterested, sheep-rearing and fishing their concerns. He came to the conclusion that if James was still eager over this, he could just send up ships to collect the tusks from the beaches which the great creatures haunted, and possibly make some small payments to local men to collect them.

So he would advise.

It had made an interesting journey, but scarcely profitable. Could he report to the monarch by letter rather than have to go all the way south to London? After all, his findings were fairly negative.

It had been an odd duty and experience for a lawyer.

9

The couple, getting on with making Craighall their comfortable and desirable home, and Thomas coping with his legal duties, were less than happy to hear from the king that he wanted more than the report sent to him regarding the Faroes. He commanded a personal interview, or audience as he put it, for fuller information.

So it had to be down to London again. And without Elizabeth's company this time, for she announced that she was pregnant again – and he certainly wanted no complications, or a miscarriage on shipboard in possibly rough seas.

At Whitehall, he informed his monarch in detail as to the Faroes situation, and advised that no purchase of the islands was necessary, the terrain being of no evident value to Scotland, and the walrms tusks available for any who cared to go and have them sawn off the creatures. All that was required was a ship's crew equipped with weapons and saws.

"Nae payments?" his money-conscious king enquired.

"No, Sire. Although some small kindness towards the local folk would be appropriate. They seem to place little or no value on the tusks."

"The mair fools them! But if they see oor men working on the dead critturs, and sawing off the ivory, they'll belike see there's moneys in it and start demanding their share. Could we no' gie them some sma' siller, for the taking o' it? A bit rent, like. Sae that ithers dinna skim the cream o' it?"

"Who pay the rent to, Sire?"

"That I dinna ken. Whae owns the land?"

"I have no notion, Your Grace. Those isles belong in name to Denmark, but seem to be regarded as of little worth. The folk of Tórshavn spoke of no lord or owner. The isles are not like Scotland or England. They are more or less empty, inland, the people independent."

"But . . . plenties o' the walrus?"

"Oh, yes."

"Then I'll get my Annie to pen a letter to her brother Christian, seeking for me a bit title to yon beaches. Tae what I can glean frae them. I'd send him a bit gift for it. To mak siccar ithers dinna tak up this o' the tusks. We'll mak thae Faroes oor consairn – forbye no' oor property. Hoo say you, Hope man?"

"It sounds a worthy project. If King Christian will agree."

"Och, if he doesna dae anything wi' thae isles, he'll be glad o' a bit gift, yon yin. And I'm his guid-brother, mind. We'll see tae it. *You* see tae the selling o' the ivory. Find oot the price tae be had. And whether thae Hansa merchants are the best market. Mebbe some ither fowk would pay better? In yon Amsterdam or Antwerp or some place. Find oot."

"If I can, Sire . . ."

"Och, that's what you're a lawyer for, is it no'? *My* lawyer. See you, Tam o' the Coogate is the Lord Advocate o' Scotland, but he's nae muckle use in maitters such as this. Ower book-learned, and nae using his wits – nae in *my* cause, that is! Though they say he feathers his ain nest weel enough! Aye, I'll mebbe can get rid o' him. Gie him mair o' a title. An earl, mebbe? He'd go for that. And mak you the Lord Advocate. Hoo say you?"

"I, I have no ambition to replace Sir Thomas, Your

Grace. So long as I can serve you. And live full life. And be laird of Craighall."

"Aye, my modest mannie! That's you, is it? But och, I can use you, use you fine. In no' just this o' the ivory. In muckle else, I judge. You and Geordie Heriot and the India Company. A law-man and a money-man and a king! That could mak a richt guid combine, no? Aye, we'll see. But, meantime, you find oot the best market and price for thae tusks. There's plenties made oot o' ivory, mind. In this palace, forbye. Statues, footstools, even a chair or two. And caskets. Jewel-boxes for the women. Aye, even chessmen."

"Very well, Your Grace. I will test the market. Whether walrus ivory will fetch as good a price as that of Indian elephants, I know not. But, for this of the Faroes and King Christian, it will be necessary to go to Denmark and see him. Letters will scarcely serve. And if I go to Copenhagen, I am none so far from the Hansa town of Lübeck on the Baltic Sea. So there I can learn the prices for the ivory."

"Dae that. You'd best go to the merchants first, mind, to ken the right value, afore you see yon Christian. But dinna mak ower much o' this o' the ivory tae him. Or belike he'll learn its true worth, and keep it a' for himsel'. Or demand the mair for it. Aye, and thae Faroe Isles bit rent."

"Yes, Sire."

"The bit gift tae him? Gie him ower much and he'll ken the right value o' it a'. What'll serve for him?"

"That is hard to judge. But . . . between kings and kinsmen by marriage? Would . . . Sire, would a great diamond serve as the gift? I have links with the diamond trade in Amsterdam. A fine one, which he could present to his queen? Or sell to whom he thought best?"

"Aye, that's it. A big diamond. Frae mysel' to him. Geordie Heriot'll gie you the moneys for it. He'll add it tae my loan! Gie it as rent for that Faroes beaches. You see tae it, man."

Thomas bowed out of the presence.

So now he had another journey to make, to Amsterdam first, and then to the Baltic, to Lübeck, to discover ivory prices from the Hansa merchants. Then to Copenhagen to see King Christian over this of the Faroes. Much toing and froing, assessing and responsibility. But worth it, for his future? He might become Scotland's next Lord Advocate, chief of the entire legal system, appointer of judges and justiciars. What would Elizabeth say to that? She was not greatly interested in prestige and the like, but . . .

Leaving Elizabeth at this time of her pregnancy was troubling, but on royal duties he could not put off. He hoped that he could win home in time for her lying-in. He would make every effort to speed up his various tasks in Denmark and Lübeck; after all, he did not actually have to *go* to the Faroes. Much would depend on the availability of ships to take him to the Baltic and back.

In fact, he was able to return in ample time for the birth, always an anxious event – and to a different kind of challenge also, which as a goodish Presbyterian he felt he had to meet. This was the prosecution by the crown of six parish ministers of the Kirk on charges of no less than high treason. They had proclaimed from their pulpits that the king and his council had no authority in ecclesiastical affairs, a statement that had greatly offended the monarch who preferred the episcopal form of worship, as did most of his advisers. The six had been imprisoned in Blackness Castle, near Linlithgow, and were to be tried at that county town, but could not find any lawyers to defend them against the crown. One of the most prestigious, Sir William Oliphant, had reluctantly agreed to do so, but resiled from it after pressure was brought to bear on him.

Thomas was much concerned over this, that, whatever the offence, subjects of the monarch could not receive a fair trial for lack of defending advocates. This, he declared, made a mockery of the law of the land, and had to be contested. And since none other seemed to be prepared to act for the six ministers, he volunteered to appear for them, even though he judged that their declaration had rather been asking for trouble. But the law of the land had to be upheld. He was, after all, Advocate and Solicitor to the Kirk of Scotland. This was, he declared, his simple duty.

The trial was to be held in the palace at Linlithgow, and the prisoners were brought from Blackness. They were much impressed when they learned that they were to be represented by so renowned a defender.

However, they were less so when they discovered who their judges were to be, under no less than the Chancellor of the Realm himself, Alexander Seaton, Earl of Dunfermline, with a panel of prominent noblemen, which seemed to indicate most authoritative backing, presumably from the monarch.

The pre-trial at Linlithgow did not start auspiciously for the defenders, or for Thomas, when the panel, on the dais of the Great Hall, began proceedings by announcing that they were surprised and disappointed to perceive that these foolish and indeed treasonable parish ministers were being represented by so distinguished an advocate, whom they considered to be acting inadvisedly in this case.

Thomas replied, "Our law, my lords, provides for every charged offender to be defended in the high court by a qualified advocate. I perceive these ministers to be innocent of any offence alleged, however outspoken they may have been. This charge of high treason for stating that the monarch has no authority in ecclesiastical affairs, while perhaps unwise to be proclaimed in a church service, is not unlawful. And therefore this prosecution itself is unlawful, as was their imprisonment in Blackness Castle."

"Making treasonable statements is ever unlawful, Sir Thomas," Dunfermline declared. "They asserted that His Grace has no authority in matters ecclesiastical. This is a denial of the royal power. The king can, for instance, confirm or oppose the appointment of bishops. Can you excuse or deny that?"

"That may be so, but it was not in that context that these clergymen spoke. It was that freedom of worship is the right of every one of His Grace's subjects, whether Presbyterian, Episcopalian, Roman Catholic, or other. That is the law, and must be upheld."

"The King's Grace does not contest that. But these ministers declared that he has no authority in affairs ecclesiastical, which His Highness *has*. You cannot deny it, sir."

"Their statements were perhaps unwisely worded, yes. But they were referring to their own Church, the Presbyterian Kirk of Scotland, wherein what they averred does apply."

"That does not alter the wrongfulness of their statements. The king's authority is supreme in certain appointments."

"But not in all affairs ecclesiastical."

There were angry declarations from the panel, and fingers pointed at Thomas.

"You are of the Kirk yourself!" one shouted.

"I am. But I speak not as such, but as an exponent and upholder of the law. *I* know the law, if you do not!"

The Lord Advocate, Sir Thomas Hamilton of Binning, intervened. "I declare that if this case comes to trial in the high court, and the jury does not convict, they themselves would be liable to be tried by an Assize of Error, and their lives and fortunes would be at the mercy of the king, whose royal authority is thus challenged. Treason indeed!"

"In this I disagree with my learned friend," Thomas asserted. "In the high court, the law must prevail. And in law these ministers have committed no offence. Their statement, as regards the Kirk, is true."

"Shame on you for saying it!"

Dunfermline banged on the dais table. "This is not a court of law. But here is unsuitable talk. We are councillors of His Grace. We have heard what the Lord Advocate has to say. I declare Sir Thomas Hope in error!"

"And I second," Lord Melville cried.

"And I do not!" That was the Earl of Mar.

"Nor I," said the Earl of Cassillis.

The Chancellor shook his head. "This is not a court, I say! Only a panel of the Privy Council, to decide if it all goes to the high court or not. We have, I say, heard enough to decide on this. I call a vote."

There were fifteen of them on the dais. Thomas lost his case by nine votes against his six.

He had to bow out.

However, the fact that he, so knowledgeable in law, was against the majority decision by magnates who were not lawyers, and that majority only three in fifteen, gave pause to the proposal to prosecute the ministers. And that pause was to lengthen. Throughout the land the Presbyterian Kirk resounded with praise for Sir Thomas Hope, and not only its members but others took note and approved. This of the Linlithgow ministers had done Thomas's repute no harm.

But he wondered what the effect would be on King James. Had he damaged his standing with his liege-lord? Time would tell.

Meanwhile he had joy at Craighall. Elizabeth was delivered of another son, to be named after his father, and there was much celebration. With increasing income from his legal fees, and the flourishing of the East India Company and its shares, Thomas decided that he should purchase more land. Young Ianie would inherit Craighall, so Tammy should have a lairdship also. After some prospecting of the possibilities, he elected to buy the properties of Arnydie and Hill of Tarvit, none so far off from Craighall, Elizabeth supportive. Land-ownership had its satisfactions, this born in mankind.

A summons to London came in the spring, Thomas wondering as to his reception by the king, after the Linlithgow affair where he had supported the ministers who claimed the monarch's powers limited. Was he being sent for to be censured? Some time had elapsed since that matter.

At Whitehall, James did not mention those ministers, whether he had heard about them or not – and the Wisest Fool was usually remarkedly well informed. What he wanted was advice about Tam o' the Coogate, Sir Thomas Hamilton the Lord Advocate. He was, in James's opinion, acting unsuitably. The Lord Advocate had the privilege not exactly of appointing the judges of the high court, that was the king's prerogative, but of nominating their names for the royal approval or otherwise. And, according to James, he was nominating the wrong men. What was to be done about Hamilton?

This presented a poser for Thomas. He and Hamilton were not in any way friends, but nor were they foes.

Hamilton was an able lawyer, and had indeed been appointed a Lord of Session, as Lord Drumcairn, but had resigned this to become Lord Advocate. And he was married to George Heriot's sister, which was no disadvantage to his prospects. He had been one of the commissioners to treat of the union of Scotland and England in 1604.

The only weakness in Hamilton's situation that Thomas could think of was his rumoured predisposition to side with the loftier parties where possible in court cases, a sort of sycophancy towards the aristocracy, which might well indicate an ambition for higher personal status. If the king wanted to replace him as Lord Advocate and nominator of judges, why not offer him a peerage, and say that he could use his talents in the House of Lords? That would probably tempt him. He might even be useful there, in London, on the monarchy's behalf. He had inherited the small property of Binning, in Linlithgowshire, and had recently bought the small castle of Garleton in Haddingtonshire, near Thomas's own farm of New Mains. Why not create him Lord Binning, or this of Garleton? That would please. And he to relinquish the office of Lord Advocate.

"Aye, and mak you Lord Advocate in his room?"

"Ah no, Sire. Not that. It would be too . . . manifest. With myself Advocate and Solicitor for the Kirk, and Hamilton an Episcopalian! Some other for Lord Advocate. Perhaps Sir William Oliphant?"

"If you say so, man. But I see you as a guid Lord Advocate. And like to nominate the right judges."

"I could always advise Your Grace on this informally. If so you would wish."

"Aye, dae that. But keep in mind this o' the Advocacy for yoursel'. Would this Oliphant serve weel eneuch meantime?"

"I judge that he would, Sire."

"Send him doon tae me, then. And I'll hae a look at him. I could move him itherwhere, if *you* want it."

"You are kind, Your Grace."

"Is it kind to ken what's what?" James changed the subject. "I hear you've been buying mair lands. In yon Fife."

"Ah, yes, Sire. It seemed wise to put what moneys I could afford into land. For my children, one day, if for naught else."

"Ooh aye. Wise eneuch. Land aye bides secure, unlike mankind! I hae to permit it, mind, under the Great Seal. For a' Scots land is mine, in name leastwise. You'll ken that, as a lawyer. Sae, I ken your buying."

"Your Grace must have a good memory, to remember all land sales that you have to endorse."

"Och, I mind those o' my freends."

"You honour me, Sire."

"I *trust* you, Hope man – that's what. Whaur I dinna trust yon Tam o' the Coogate! Or no' that far, onyway. Why I'd see *you* Lord Advocate. I'll mind this o' making him Lord Binning. And Oliphant, was it? The mannie to mak Lord Advocate, until you're ready to be it."

"I have over-many interests and responsibilities as it is, Sire. As you know, with the East India Company and the diamond trade on the Continent, and land matters here at home. But one day, perhaps . . ."

"Aye. And mind tae advise me as to thae judges. *They*, when they sit in the courts, represent me, mind. *I'm* the fount o' justice, I was tell't at my coronation. Sae it's gey important that they're the richt men, no' jist Tam o' the Coogate's freends."

"I shall not forget, Sire."

They spoke of the Faroes and the walrus tusks and ivory trade. Sir Andrew Wood, the second of that name, was seeing to this, and profitably.

James still had said nothing about those ministers at Linlithgow.

10

Thomas had not realised what his defence of the six
ministers at Linlithgow would run him into, however
unsuccessful it had been. Now, innumerable legal disputes,
whether over land and boundaries, stipends and tithes,
church buildings, and even graveyards, were referred to
him and kept him busy indeed. He was, of course, Advocate
and Solicitor to the Kirk, but much that was a deal less vital
and important than official work was now notified to him
for his guidance, and a great many of the nearly fourteen
hundred parishes in the land produced a seemingly unending catalogue of problems and contentions, in especial in
affairs with the local lairds. It became all but his principal
preoccupation, little as he desired it, and indeed had him
wondering whether he ought to resign this Kirk position.
But he had a real concern for the ministers and their
parishioners, as representing the people of the land, who
were all too apt to be at the mercy of grasping lairds and
nobles, so that he was ever taking up their causes – which,
needless to say, did not commend him to the land-owning
fraternity – this while he was becoming a landowner
himself. Elizabeth sought to advise him somewhat in this
clash of interests.

On another tack, King James did effect the project of
creating Thomas Hamilton Lord Binning, and giving him
tasks in the House of Lords; and this left the Lord Advocate's position free for the appointment of Sir William

Oliphant, somewhat to that modest man's surprise. Thomas was to advise him on the appointment of judges, this with the monarch's own suggestions.

The matter of the Faroes and the ivory was much in James's mind. Andrew Wood was to see to the actual gleaning of the tusks, having the necessary ships. But the monarch was concerned that King Christian would get to hear of it and to realise what he was missing. So Thomas was to go to Copenhagen again and arrange, if possible, a rent for those beaches, so that the rights should be James's and his only. At the same time, he was to discover where there might be another market for the ivory, to compete with the prices offered by the Hansa merchants.

Thomas wondered why Andrew Wood could not have done this, but could not ask it of the king. After all, he had the ships.

Another voyage then, eastwards again, by the royal command. But a call at Amsterdam first, for surely the East India Company would be the best source of information about ivory, this, to be sure, from elephants' tusks. Was that a superior sort to the walrus variety? He had much to find out, such as the most profitable uses for the material, other than chessmen, beads, rosaries, statues and the like. Mosaics of ivory were in the catacombs, James had declared.

At Amsterdam he learned a lot. Walrus tusks were inferior in quality and durability to the elephants', as well as smaller – although even so they could reach three feet in length. But there was indeed a market for them, for the Indian and African variety were scarce and expensive to obtain. There were thousands of walrus in the Faroes, and presumably more still in Iceland. How to convince King Christian to lease the beaches to James, without him recognising that he would be better exploiting them himself?

Thomas racked his wits over this, and came to the conclusion that the competition with elephants had to be the answer; and that Scots merchants were unwilling to pay the higher price for them, which was true enough. That must serve. Was it enough to convince Christian that it was worth his while to rent out the beaches rather than having Danish ships going to collect the ivory? A bird in the hand worth two in the bush, as it were? Thomas could but try.

At Copenhagen he had little difficulty in persuading the Danish monarch to grant a lease of the Faroes beaches, these sufficiently far away and hitherto valueless, and he with no thought of seeking to trade in ivory, whereas he could certainly use the rental. Thomas was able to strike a good deal for the Scots trio, the king, George Heriot and himself. He left Copenhagen well satisfied.

Now to Lübeck to see those Hansa merchants there. He sometimes wondered why they chose this Baltic port to base themselves, although he recognised that it, so near to Hamburg by canal, could serve the Russias and far eastern lands, as well as the west and the rest of Europe.

There he spoke with the merchants over this of the ivory; and not only the Hansa ones but the local traders. He discovered that the former deliberately offered high prices, and not only for ivory, this in order to keep the value up, and corner the market so that *they* could charge the more themselves for products, a shrewd operation. But enquiries revealed no trade in *walrus* tusks. Should he approach them directly on this? Or seek a different market? Thomas, rightly or wrongly, was wary of the Hanseatic League, those expert dealers. He judged that they would almost certainly outwit him, and grab this tusk trade for themselves. He might well do better elsewhere.

So he travelled west to Hamburg, and there met a different sort of trader, these catering for a much more modest but wider forum. He found his sample tusks arousing much interest. These might have other destinations for the ivory than the Hansa ones, less lofty perhaps. But they claimed to be able to reach a great range of buyers. This was what Thomas was looking for. He was not long in coming to terms with them, they as well content as was he. He could return to Copenhagen, seal his compact with King Christian, and be for home.

It occurred to him that he was becoming as much trader as lawyer.

All was arranged satisfactorily, Christian entirely co-operative. And Sir Andrew Wood, when Thomas saw him, equally so; and appreciative of his share of the profits.

Those profits were accumulating, along with fees from his ever-increasing legal services; and turning silver and gold into land remained Thomas's concern. He was ever seeking word of suitable properties for sale, especially, but not only, in Fife, and these last as near to Craighall as might be. The king had created that a barony. Now Thomas wished it to be a worthy one. He had heard that the laird of Pitscottie, near to Ceres, and Pitfirrane further west in the Dunfermline area, had died leaving no direct heir; and it occurred to him that the elderly widow might well be glad to be relieved of the responsibilities for this quite large estate if she could be life-rented suitably on the property. He went to see her at the mansion of Pitfirrane, and found her frail and depressed, worried about the estates to maintain, and was only too glad to sell much of it to Thomas. She also mentioned the lesser estate of Baldovie, near to Dundee, with its mill, which had also belonged to her husband. Would Sir Thomas be interested in purchasing that?

Thomas was, and saw his lands growing satisfactorily.

Also satisfactory was the fact that Elizabeth was pregnant again, and nearing delivery. She bore him a girl, this time, after a comparatively easy birth, and to rejoicing; they named her after her mother. Sadly the infant died after only a few weeks. The couple had to realise that life could not be all success and satisfaction.

They were still mourning the loss of little Lisa when word arrived from brother Harry in Amsterdam. His diamond business, there and at Antwerp, had greatly prospered and he was becoming wealthy, and indeed being appointed to the ruling board of the East India Company no less. He had married a Dutch lady named Adele, and she had just given birth to a son, another Harry. He wrote urging his brother to come and visit them, meet wife and child, and see the handsome new house he had built, just off the Leidseplein.

It seemed to Thomas that this might be a good way of helping Elizabeth to get over the death of Lisa. Also it might be good policy to invest some of his earnings in either the diamond trade or the East India Company, or both. They would make a trip to the Netherlands, and they would take Ian with them, but not Tam.

They did not have to wait long for a ship to sail them to Amsterdam, from Leith.

Elizabeth was good about not allowing her depression to spoil their travel.

Thomas enjoyed being back in the Netherlands, very different from Scotland in so many ways, in its people as well as in its scenery, Amsterdam's markets, innumerable canals and colourful buildings. Harry's new house, on one of the canals, was splendid indeed, all but a palace by Scots standards. They found his Adele plump, quite motherly and an excellent hostess, and her hospitality almost overmuch, a provider of huge meals. Her English was scanty, but that was the only drawback, and she made up for it with gales of laughter, Harry clearly adoring her.

Whether it was her feeding of him or otherwise, Harry was becoming heavy as to build, unlike Thomas who was fairly slenderly made; and the difference had Adele exclaiming that Elizabeth could not be feeding him adequately, and that she would have to make up for this, protesting when he left portions on his overfull platters. Young Ian pleased her with his remarkable appetite.

Harry was interested to hear of his brother's purchasing of lands, he having no such grand ambitions of land-ownership, although he was even more prosperous than Thomas. He used his wealth to buy fine furnishings and hangings and eastern carpets for his huge houses – for he had more than one – statuary for the gardens, to employ servants, gardeners, coachmen, handymen and the like. He even had a magnificent barge, all but a floating palace, to sail the network of canals that criss-crossed that level and waterlogged land, this staffed by cooks as well as crews, to provide for Adele's standards of catering.

So the visitors were taken on much water travel, which greatly pleased Ian. In that flat scene there was a great sameness about the prospects, windmills and church spires, far and wide, being the main items to catch the eye under the great skies. Elizabeth indeed declared that she had never been so aware of the sky above as when she was in the Low Countries, both by day and by night, the differing cloud formations, the towering cumulus and the level stratus, these last rivalling the outspread landscape with its endless gleam of waters. After Scotland with its mountains and hills and glens, it made vastly different viewing.

Harry was strong for Thomas to invest more in the East India Company, he declaring that this was where the future lay, now that the Spaniards' fleets had been largely nullified. There was so much to be won from all the east, and Africa, as well as the Indies, unending wealth which only awaited exploiting. Two brothers could not have been more different, and had such diverse ideas as to money and its uses. But Thomas did buy a further batch of company shares.

Harry was eager to take Thomas and Elizabeth to visit the new property he had bought in the south, and to prove that his brother was not the only Hope who could purchase lands. With his Scots upbringing, he had long pined for hills and vales in this land of levels and water; and he had found a place far off, indeed one hundred and fifty miles away, which satisfied this yearning. The Netherlands had that rather extraordinary peninsula-like extension, down between Belgian Liège and German Cologne, this narrow and so different from the rest of the Dutch countryside, a terrain of green hills and open woodlands, valleys and lakes, the province and duchy of Limburg. There he had found a small mansion with sheep-farming uplands, which provided him with the scenery and prospects he liked – whatever Adele thought of it.

No barges were able to take them there, so it had to be horseback, which suited Elizabeth and Thomas very well, Adele less so, she no horsewoman, this delaying their progress somewhat; but it was interesting country, after the flats and polders, and there were no complaints.

It took them three days to reach Linden Chapelle, at the

pace they had to go, the country getting ever hillier and more attractive, at least to the Scots. They could see why Harry liked it.

The small estate was really a cattle farm, into which Harry had imported blackface sheep from the Lammermuirs of Lothian. These seemed to thrive well here, three hundred miles south of their home grazings as it was, with no heather nor bracken but richer grasses. So they now had mutton for their evening meal, something they had not tasted in the Netherlands hitherto, where beef and poultry and fish were the staples.

Harry was quite proud of this little imitation of Lowland Scotland that he had conjured up, and his sheep mingled with the Friesian cattle happily enough. Thomas asked whether they grew less heavy fleeces here in this warmer clime, but his brother knew not. It was not for the wool that he kept them.

Adele approved of the mutton at least, and they had soup and stew and chops while they were at Linden Chapelle. Harry asked whether Thomas had ever come across *smoked* mutton? If the meat could be so treated, to keep for periods, then he would take supplies back north to Amsterdam.

His brother knew not. He had never heard of smoked mutton. But if other meat and fish could be so preserved, he did not see why not. Try it.

They spent a pleasant three days in the Limburg hills, but Thomas was beginning to worry about getting back to Scotland and his many duties, and Elizabeth was anxious that all was well with Tammy. She believed that she was pregnant once more. Harry and Adele would have had them stay longer. But it had to be Amsterdam and a ship for them, with urgings to the other couple to come to Scotland soon and see how the Hope lands were growing there.

Elizabeth gave birth to another son, whom they named William – but with some anxiety, for the child was, like his late sister, born feeble, and the physicians shook heads over him.

Thomas had meanwhile embarked on a new project involving land and building, this in Edinburgh. Much of his legal duties had to be dealt with there, where were the law courts and advocates' chambers, and where the Scots parliament frequently sat. And with the family growing, and entertainment having to be provided for clients and colleagues, these often quite lofty in status, something better than Todd's Close, off the High Street, was called for. These days the Cowgate, formerly just a sort of lane parallel with that main street and leading from the Grass-market to Holyrood, was being developed as an up-market housing and business thoroughfare; and Elizabeth thought that it should be the site of their city residence. Hamilton, Lord Binning, lived there – he whom the monarch referred to as Tam o' the Coogate – and not a few other lords and lairds and prominent folk were making it the site of their town-houses.

So Thomas bought a plot of ground therein, and ordered a fine tenement of four storeys and an attic to be erected, the two lower storeys to be available for market-stalls and traders, the upper floors to be commodious and bright, with good windows and a wide stairway, handsomely furnished, and including a chamber for interviewing clients and also a clerks' room.

This development, his land-hunger as Elizabeth called it, led him to further purchases in this Edinburgh and the Lothians area. That year he bought the lands of Granton, along the Forth shore west of Leith port; Edmonstone and Prestongrange to the east; Kerse in Stirlingshire; and Mertoun in the Merse. He saw those near Edinburgh as an investment, for the capital city was ever growing, and would continue to do so undoubtedly, and the land around become ever more valuable. Not that Craighall was going to be just some sort of summer house – that was their *home*, and should remain so. But, one day, their children would require lands and houses.

This of children was both a joy and a sorrow. For happy as they were with Ian and Tammy, little William, like his sister, did not live long. Were they to have to get used to the sad task of burying offspring? Elizabeth's womb was receptive, but . . .

Thomas received another royal command, a summons to London again, his advice sought. This he could have done without. Surely James had a sufficiency of well-qualified advisers there, in matters of law, as in all else? But he had to go.

The king was off hunting at Windsor, as so often, so it was up Thames to that great establishment, where he was greeted with royal reproaches that he had been so long in appearing – although he had not delayed in setting out, nor on the long journey on horseback.

"Hope man," he was told, "it's this o' yon Tam o' the Coogate. Binning, I've made him, mind. He's back in Scotland. Gien up the appointment in the Hoose o' Lords. Vicky o' Lennox says he's seeking the position o' Lord Clerk

Register; the mannie whae had it, Skene o' Curriehill, deid. I'm no' richt sure what yon means or what he daes. You'll ken. But if *he* wants it, it maun be o' some guid, some worth."

"It is, in effect, Clerk to the Privy Council, Sire – but more than just a clerk. A member of the council itself, who instructs the clerks and advises the other counsellors. Also approves of, or otherwise, justices of the peace."

"Say you so? I jalouse yon's a richt gainfu' employ, no? Many'll pay weel to be justices!"

Thomas did not comment on that.

"Should I let him hae this o' the Clerk Register? He's richt ambitious, the man. He'll be wanting ever mair. Secretary o' State, belike. Hoo say you?"

This was difficult for Thomas to answer. He did not want to seem to act against Hamilton. He recognised that he was an able man, with a shrewd mind, and could probably serve the monarch in Scotland well enough. But, on the other hand, overmuch power might not be for the realm's good. Duke Ludovick was wary of him . . .

"It is not for such as myself to say, Sire, another lawyer . . ."

"That's why I'm asking you!"

"Yes. This of the Lord Clerk Register. If he seeks it, it might keep him happy, and be nowise harmful. Secretary of State, however, might be . . . different. But Sir Alexander Hay is that."

"Aye, but he's being made Keeper o' the Privy Seal, and a Senator o' the College o' Justice. Sae he canna be Secretar o' State tae."

"In that case, Sire, is there aught against Hamilton becoming it?"

"That's what I'm asking o' *you*! You maun ken him better than maist."

Thomas shook his head. What was he to advise? If the Duke of Lennox thought otherwise. "I know him only as a fellow-lawyer, Your Grace. Not as a statesman. But I have much respect for the duke's opinions."

"Aye. I'ph'mm. We'll see. He can be Lord Clerk Register meantimes. And we'll think on this o' Secretar o' State. It's richt difficult tae ken in a' these maitters."

"I regret being of no real help to Your Grace. But . . ."

Thomas was thankful to escape from Windsor. This of advising the monarch for or against others was not to his pleasure. It was different in a court of law, where an advocate represented one appellant and therefore opposed the other. But, behind the scenes as it were, counselling his liege-lord was not what he would have chosen.

James, however, had more than this of Hamilton to put to him, thus absent from his northern kingdom. The General Assembly of the Kirk of Scotland was due to hold its annual conference shortly; and James wanted guidance on whom to appoint as his Lord High Commissioner to open and oversee it, since he certainly was not going to himself. The monarch leaned towards bishops, as did Ludovick of Lennox, but his representative for the occasion ought not to be an Episcopalian. Whom might be appoint?

Thomas also worshipped in that direction. He suggested that the Chancellor, Alexander Seton, Earl of Dunfermline, would make a worthy and authoritative High Commissioner.

"But he's ower far to the richt, man," the monarch asserted. "Yon Seton even went tae Rome in his studies, I mind. The Kirk wouldna tak kindly tae the likes o' him."

"I think that it might, Sire. He changed his mind, after Rome, and came to the conclusion that the reformed faith was for him. What he saw at the Vatican must have affected him. And, as often, when a man changes his mind, he can well swing the more strongly in the other direction. I have heard that the earl is approved of by the divines just *because* of making that move leftwards. He would be well received as Your Highness's Commissioner, I judge."

"Say you so? Then Dunfermline let it be. As Chancellor he presides fine ower the Scots parliaments. Sae he'll dae the same ower this Assembly. And keep thae dreich preachers in order! Send you him doon tae me, and I'll tell him the way o' it. He was Seton o' Fyvie afore I made him earl, I mind."

"Yes, Sire. A brother of the Lord Seton who became Earl of Wintoun. From Lothian, none so far from my Prestongrange."

"He'll hae a task keeping thae Melvilles, Andro and James, doon. Richt dour critturs them!"

"No doubt they have their virtues, Sire."

"I doot it! They ca'd me the Lord's silly vassal! I'll no' forget that! Dunfermline'll hae to be richt severe wi' them and their like. You'll attend wi' him, will you?"

"If so you say, Sire. But I do not think that he will need me!"

"Mebbe no'. But nae herm in ha'ing your support."

So Thomas had to attend a General Assembly of the Kirk ministers, in the West Bow of Edinburgh, off the Lawnmarket, something he had not had occasion to do hitherto, this in the company of Dunfermline. It was an experience he was not likely to forget. Many of the divines were apt to be dominant in their own pulpits, and did not change their style here, argumentative and dictatorial. Assembly, or bringing together as the word meant, it might be termed, but togetherness was scarcely the prevailing ambience. Keeping any sort of order was all but impossible, however requiring of the Almighty had been the opening prayers for guidance, direction and blessing. Bishops might become haughty and authoritative, but not apt to reach such levels of strident assertion as here was attained. Moderator as the chairman might be styled, and needfully so, his quelling of the discordance of the proceedings was less than evident.

Thomas was thankful when it was at last over – and it took three days – as clearly was Dunfermline. He took Elizabeth and the children back to Craighall, declaring that he hoped that the king would not command him to attend another General Assembly.

Thomas had an unexpected visitor shortly thereafter, George Heriot, the royal banker. He had now transferred his base from Edinburgh to London, but still retained a house and office in the north. The monarch had long been heavily in debt to him. Heriot knew that Thomas had made that great survey of the lands and estates of Scotland that paid dues to the crown; and now the king was wondering whether the funds that he so greatly needed could be raised from some of these, through further legal dues and taxes. James would be grateful indeed if such requirement could be established.

Thomas agreed that use might be made of the survey he had conducted, to the king's benefit, however unpopular this might be with the present landholders. What was being proposed?

Heriot said that if he, Sir Thomas, had kept notes of that survey of his, especially of the former Church lands, he and Lord Binning, Heriot's cousin, might use these to improve greatly the royal revenues, to the monarch's gratitude and to their own advantage.

Thomas pondered. There might be truth in this, and of

value to the crown. But what of the lairds? Any royal exploitation of it all might make him and Binning very unpopular with the landowners – and he was now a size-able landowner himself. He might even discover some crown dues applicable to his own properties. Was his allegiance to the monarchial welfare and interests to make him the foe of his fellows? Did Binning concern himself with the like?

He delved among his old survey papers, and came across quite a lot that could be of worth to the crown.

He decided that he ought to consult Hamilton. So he went west to Monkland, in mid-Lanarkshire, that man's seat. He was somewhat doubtfully received. But on the issue being explained to him, the other thawed, perceiving that if the two most prominent lawyers in Scotland worked together on this, they ought to achieve something worth while.

They pored over Thomas's papers, and picked out not a few items that might be of value, Hamilton taking notes, voluminous notes, especially interested in the temporal-ities of former Church lands – and the Kirk had been rich indeed in such. They came to the conclusion that there was ample here, especially in those sasines and tempor-alities, that could be acted upon for the crown's benefit, which all the centuries of clerics had accumulated, rights that dying landlords had offered to Holy Church for prayers to be said for their immortal souls in perpetuity. The Reformation had transferred most of these either to the crown or to new landholders; but much remained, as it were in limbo, as Heriot had guessed. Here was ground to be tilled.

Later, the three of them went over it all carefully and in detail, and worked on how they should proceed with the task they had set themselves. Would James Stewart be duly grateful, even if many lords and lairds were not? Binning would go down to London to inform the monarch on it all.

12

When Hamilton returned to Scotland in due course, he came back a happy man. He had achieved his ambition, long held, to become not just a lord but an earl. He was now Earl of Melrose, that famed town and abbey near where he had bought the property of Drumcairn. He was, however, vague as to what the rewards might be for Thomas and George Heriot. Perhaps he had not enquired.

The Hopes' new town-house in Edinburgh's Cowgate was now completed, and the family could use it when they were in the city – which Thomas often was. And there, inevitably, he saw much of Tam o' the Coogate, Earl of Melrose, now judging himself as the most distinguished resident, his wife, Margaret, a daughter of James Borthwick of Newbyres, acting the countess with style. This had Thomas's Elizabeth demanding when *she* was going to be elevated to a like status, although she was perfectly content to be Lady Hope of Craighall. Her husband had no ambitions in that direction, seeing the House of Lords as requiring too much time to be spent in London, and being a peer of no advantage in his work and life.

His links with the East India Company and the diamond trade called for frequent visits to Amsterdam. It was good to see brother Harry and his growing family, he now one of the major figures there, and become all but a Dutchman, his children speaking better Dutch than English. Elizabeth could not accompany him as often as she would have liked, because of the children.

Now, with Hamilton raised to an earldom, it was unsuitable that he should continue to be the Lord Clerk Register, although he remained a member of the Privy Council. Thomas took on that added responsibility, over and above being King's Advocate, a personal appointment of the monarch's, distinct from being *Lord* Advocate of Scotland. James wanted him to remain in close touch, because of those ever more valuable East India Company shares, and the diamonds. The king was beginning to show his age, but was no less concerned with financial problems, he claiming that his Queen Anne was extravagance personified, she even now having her own palace built at Greenwich, designed by Inigo Jones.

James had declared that he would return to his northern kingdom every three years; but in fact he had not done so, and it was fourteen years after he went south to mount Queen Elizabeth's throne, during which time Thomas and Elizabeth had increased their family, before he made the journey north again, in the spring of 1617.

There was much opposition in London to his going. He was determined to travel in style, with a great train; but the royal treasury was, as so often, all but empty, and the expedition would be costly indeed. His English advisers, Howard, Earl of Suffolk, and Buckingham, the monarch's current favourite, even went down on their knees to plead with him not to go. But to no effect. James had made up his mind, even though partly crippled with gout and arthritis. In fact, well over a thousand courtiers, nobles and attendants escorted him, and a slow journey they all made of it, by no means taking the most direct route, diverting constantly to visit chosen locations, cities and towns, castles, mansions and abbeys, engaging in hunting, enjoying pageantry, feasting, and demanding lavish hospitality for the huge cavalcade, and making knights. By Hertford and Bedford, Huntingdon and Leicester, Nottingham and Lincoln, Doncaster and Leeds to York, he went. And on by Northallerton and Darlington to Durham and Newcastle, eventually crossing the border and the Tweed at Norham, to arrive in Edinburgh at last on 16 May, to great welcome and rejoicing by the citizenry at this return of their own Scots liege-lord.

Queen Anne, not in the best of health, did not accompany her husband.

The rejoicing in Scotland flagged somewhat when, at Holyrood, James held an Anglican Episcopalian church service, with kneeling at Communion, to the wrath of the Presbyterian divines and glarings at the bishops. As ever, the Scots flourished their divisions.

An especial welcoming session of the Scots parliament was held, the king on his throne thereat, and there was an unsuitably stormy interlude when fervent Presbyterian members made vehement protest over that choral service and the kneeling, joint occasion as it had been, the monarch tut-tutting.

On Thomas's advice, James attended an alternative Presbyterian worship at St Andrews thereafter to placate the divines, this on his way to Falkland for his favourite activity of hunting red deer, the like of which the smaller fallow deer of England could by no means rival. James had greatly missed this more taxing sport in the south, for however ungainly he was in the saddle, as in so much else, he was a keen horseman.

At Falkland, Thomas discovered from his liege-lord that the King of Denmark, Annie's brother, wanted to increase the rental previously negotiated for the lease of the Faroes beaches. When Thomas enquired how much, he expressed disappointment that James had considered this too large a sum, declaring that the ivory therefrom would quite quickly repay the extra outlay. On the king's head-shakings, he added that George Heriot, who on matters financial could not be rivalled, was much in favour of this, the ivory market being assured and the price ever growing. King Christian's requirements were not exorbitant in the circumstances.

Thomas suggested that a new approach should be made, and when the monarch wagged his head, be-hatted as always, proposed that he himself might go to see Christian, and if possible take George Heriot with him. The latter had spoken about increased trading possibilities with both Hamburg and the Hansa merchants at Lübeck, this for Lammermuir wool, timber, whisky, salted meats, even coal. Scotland's commerce with the Baltic lands, England's too for that matter, could be much enhanced – and the royal revenues with it.

James promptly accepted that, and agreed that they both could go, with the royal authority.

So, after seeking to fit in an absence of possibly three weeks in his busy schedule, and persuading Heriot to do likewise, it was one more voyage across the Norse Sea, heading for Hamburg and Lübeck first, and then for Copenhagen or Elsinore, wherever the King of Denmark was to be found, new ground and waters for Jinglin' Geordie. He made an excellent companion. Fortunately there was never any lack of merchant ships sailing for Hamburg and the Baltic from Leith.

It all made a successful trip, in more than the ivory connection, Thomas taking whisky casks with them, as a speculation, and finding the contents going down well with the schnapps- and vodka-drinking fraternity, Heriot negotiating orders for this, to his profit. They found that the Roman Catholic Church was the principal destination for the ivory. It flourished, despite the Reformation, all over Europe, as did the Eastern Orthodox faith, prominent here also. Both were interested in ivory for altars, fonts, lecterns and decorations, providing no lack of openings for the trade.

King Christian was well pleased to see Thomas back again, with his companion, anticipating advantage therefrom. A revised rental for the Faroes beaches was negotiated, and other trading opportunities discussed. Any financial increase was welcomed, for Denmark was involved in a long-running war of sorts, seeking to bring nearby Sweden under sway, a costly drain on resources. The king wondered whether the great isles beyond the Faroes, Iceland, even Greenland, both nominally part of Denmark, could be exploited for ivory, walrus undoubtedly being prevalent there also. Thomas had to declare that the Faroes were capable of supplying all the ivory presently called for, but these distant parts would be remembered. Greenland was known to be the largest island in all the world, but its nearness to the Arctic ice meant that its waters were not navigable for much of the year.

Meetings with Copenhagen's and other merchants were arranged, and trade with Scottish products discussed, Heriot in his element, Thomas ever learning. The Danish dealers were in fact well pleased with this possible development, for they had long been more or less at the mercy of the Hanseatic League's monopoly, this dominating the markets. They saw direct imports and exports with Scotland and England much to their benefit, and this of the two

Scots visitors having King James's royal backing, plus that of King Christian, of real advantage.

Thomas recognised that he was becoming almost as much merchant-venturer as lawyer, and found no real fault with that. It would all undoubtedly add to his substance, and enable him to buy more land, still very much his objective. Was he over eager in this concern? Elizabeth had hinted at it. He had quite a few other landed purchases in view. Hamilton was ever at the same and, at the back of Thomas's mind, he did not want to be outdone by his colleague and rival. That land survey of his had made him keenly aware of the great amount of prime property there was in Scotland; and a substantial stake in it was to be aimed for. His wife was pregnant once more, so there would be no lack of Hope offspring to be provided with estates. The more children the better, they both felt. Was that the Scots clan spirit surfacing?

George Heriot was anxious not to be away from home for overlong, as was he, in this respect. The other had married Alison Primrose, the daughter of another lawyer, James Primrose, Clerk to the Privy Council, and so a colleague of Thomas, who was now Lord Clerk Register. She too was pregnant; and getting back to her side was a priority. Eliabeth was at an earlier stage than Alison. So this Scandinavian visit must not be prolonged, however much Thomas would have liked to explore the Baltic coasts further.

And it was back to tragedy. Alison had gone into premature labour, and died in childbirth, the infant with her, this eight days before. Heriot was heartbroken, a man devastated. He blamed himself for being away when she most needed him.

Elizabeth was nearing another delivery herself. But

having already produced seven babies she was not unduly fearful, although three had died young, and there was always the dread that this might happen again. Prayers were said for her, and for their grieving friend. In due course she gave birth to a healthy daughter, whom they named Mary.

Thomas meantime became involved in what amounted to almost a battle with his liege-lord. The financially troubled monarch, seeking to cope with his wife's spendings, as well as his own, and already in deep debt to George Heriot, devised a scheme to help with this, a system of royal monopolies. James declared that it was to encourage trade and manufactures, for the realm's benefit; but in fact it was largely to line his own empty pockets. Tradesmen and merchants, if they paid a sum, a substantial sum, to him, were to be given the sole right to make or sell certain goods and services, and to charge what they pleased for them. They were to be able to call themselves purveyors to the king: tailors to the king, soap-makers to the king, leather-dressers to the king, and so on. There was no lack of contestants for these privileges, vying with each other as to the amounts paid to the monarch.

When Thomas heard of this, he was more than doubtful as to its legality, at least in Scots law. Freedom to buy and sell, barter and compete, was an accepted right of the citizen, and this of monopolies appeared to be contrary to that right. The monarch was not above the law, whatever he devised, and Thomas would have to tell him so. There was nothing to prevent him appointing traders to the king, but that must not give them sole rights, and to fix prices. He had to write to James, however tactfully, to emphasise this. It was almost certainly the same in English law.

He got no reply from London; but no doubt the king consulted his English lawyers also, and would be told the like. James went on appointing purveyors to the king, but these could hold no monopoly. It was not the way for Thomas to gain royal favour, but he saw it as his simple duty. However, the king was still very much aware of the debt he owed over that survey of Scottish lands, and the royal dues that he was gaining therefrom, and was not in any position to demonstrate disapproval of his Lord Clerk Register.

Thomas had a visit from the representative of that other monarch with whom he had been in touch, Christian of Denmark. A Danish envoy came from London to seek advice on the matter of Greenland, assuming that Thomas would be knowledgeable as to this because of his links with France. Greenland, well north and west of the Faroes and of Iceland, was claimed by Denmark as an appendage, semi-Arctic as it was, although the last vestiges of the warm Gulf Stream lessened its chill. It was, in effect, one vast plateau, many hundreds of miles long, with mountains rising to twice the height of any in Scotland, or even Norway. Its inhabitants were the Inuit, or Eskimos; but there had long been a sprinkling of Danish settlers, descendants of the venturesome Vikings, and these exploited the excellent cod-fishing and the sealing, sealskins being ever in demand. But Greenland was much nearer to Canada than not only to Denmark but to the Danish Faroes and Iceland; and now the French in Canada were claiming it as theirs. Christian, well aware of Thomas's expertise in international law, and knowing his links with France and his French mother, sought his guidance as to this of Canada.

In fact, Thomas knew little about Greenland and its

history, and imagined that there were very few in Scotland who were better informed. But certain of the Glasgow shipmasters who traded with Nova Scotia might inform him. Even better, perhaps, was the king's Master of Requests for Scotland, Sir William Alexander of Menstrie, who had to all intents founded and colonised the peninsula on French Canada's coast, formerly called Acadia but named by him Nova Scotia, or New Scotland, this to the opposition of the French. No one in Scotland was more likely to put Thomas in the picture over French Canada, and possibly to some extent Greenland, than he.

So Thomas rode up-Forth to near Stirling, to the quite small castle of Menstrie, set below the Ochil Hills, a modest seat indeed for so notable a man. Sir William was entirely helpful. He declared that although Nova Scotia was now Scottish, or rather belonged to the United Kingdom, the rest of Canada, or such of its vast area as had been colonised, was French, or claimed by France. He did not think that the French had any designs on Greenland, however near their Canada, no doubt seeing it as but Arctic desert. King Christian could probably remain unconcerned. But who knew what might develop, as French settlement in Canada grew?

Was there anything of real value to be gained from Greenland's vast and distant territory? Thomas wondered. Presumably the French did not know of such, or they would probably have sought to take it over ere this. Alexander judged that there could be. He had heard that there were great herds of musk oxen, and the skins of polar bears, as well as the seals, were prized. The whale oil and blubber was ever useful – and there would be this of the ivory. But it was the cod- and halibut-fishing in which the Greenland Sea was so rich. And, of course, the ice of its glaciers and fjords enabled the catches to be kept and stored indefinitely. The Danes would be foolish to let the French take over there. Denmark, Norway, Sweden and Finland had much greater numbers of ships than had France. They should protect the territory, King Christian should be advised, and make it clear to France that they would do so.

Thomas had the information he wanted, and would pass it on.

13

It was early next year that Thomas received a peremptory command to attend the court at London, this not from the king but from his new favourite, George Villiers, son of a Leicestershire knight, whom he had made Duke of Buckingham, Master of the Horse, and Lord High Admiral of England. Puzzled by this as he was, he could not refuse what amounted to a royal command. Reluctantly he made the journey south.

At Whitehall he was shocked by the change in King James. Now in his fifty-ninth year, he had suddenly become much older-looking and doddery, vague in his manner, and returning to his bed at any hour of the day. Prince Charles, a somewhat shy although good-looking young man, unlike his sire, was now in his twenty-fifth year, and had a slight stammer to his speech. He was having to act for James on most occasions – or at least nominally so, for *he* appeared to be under the influence of this Duke of Buckingham, who in effect was all but ruling the land.

This George Villiers, handsome but assertive, lost no time in letting Thomas know why he had been sent for. His links with France and the Guises were known, and he spoke fluent French. He was therefore to accompany Buckingham to Saint-Germain, there to seek to arrange a marriage between the Princess Henrietta Maria, daughter of the late King Henry, and Charles, Prince of Wales. Why *him*? Thomas wondered. He was told that the Guise connection was important, he was half French, could deal with the dowry situation as a lawyer, and was known to Cardinal Richelieu, whom he had met with the Cardinal of Lorraine, now dead. Buckingham did not say so, but Thomas was aware that he had previously tried to contrive a marriage with the Spanish Infanta, this without success; so now this French venture. King James seemed to approve of it, so Thomas could not decline. There did seem to be some disapproval of the match in England, with fears of a possible Catholic domination of the scarcely strong-minded young Charles, whose elder brother Henry, who had died some twelve years earlier, had been a more assertive character.

Thomas did not much like Buckingham, or reports of him, allegedly arrogant of nature. But at James's urging he had to go along with the mission. He was saddened at the king's obviously grievously deteriorating state of health. There was no delay at London, for Buckingham had been impatiently waiting for him to come south. Promptly they set off from the Thames for Dieppe, this seeming to be so frequently Thomas's destination, the nearest seaport to Paris. Ships were ever heading thereto.

When they reached Saint-Germain-en-Laye, the favoured royal seat, they found Henrietta Maria to be a girl of only fifteen years, not beautiful but vivacious and ready to be friendly.

Young King Louis, Henrietta's brother, or more significantly his mother, Marie de Medici, who had acted regent after the death of King Henry, seemed to take this marriage as more or less settled, and to be almost more interested in the extent and value of the dowry being arranged. Buckingham, knowing little and caring nothing of Scotland, mentioned only the lands and manors of Huntingdon,

Kimbolton and Horsham, to which Thomas added Linlithgow and its granges in Lothian, with some details. Louis, shrugging, indicated modified satisfaction.

The necessary negotiations and arrangements did not take long, and Thomas rather wondered why it had been thought necessary for him to accompany Buckingham. He was thankful to get back to his Elizabeth and family.

Only ten days after his return, however, news came from London that King James had died, at Theobalds, after a reign of thirty-six years as King of Scots, and another twenty-two as of England also, forming the United Kingdom. Charles Stewart now inherited the throne.

There came, very shortly thereafter, another summons to London, again from Buckingham in the new king's name. With no near heir to the throne, it was felt that the sooner Charles was married and his wife pregnant the better. Charles was therefore married by proxy in Paris in May that year and awaited his young bride's arrival in his kingdom.

An especial sitting of the Scots parliament had to be held to celebrate the new reign; and since the King-in-Parliament was the official designation for the Scottish assembly, the monarch had to be present on this important occasion. It was a great occasion and display was to be made of it; for the Scots had to make it clear again that it was the ancient line of the *Scottish* kings that had ascended the United Kingdom throne. Charles, who had been born in Dunfermline Palace in Fife, and still spoke with a Scottish accent, was very proud of his venerable lineage dating back longer than any other royal line in Christendom, and was prone to emphasise this, the ancient sennachies claiming that it went back right to Noah and the Flood. Nevertheless dissension was expressed over religious matters, the vehement Presbyterians concerned, as were the Puritans in England. Charles had inherited from his father the belief in the divine right of kings; and, unassuming as he was in manner and attitude, held strongly to this royal claim, which the nonconformists and their supporters denied. The parliament grew rowdy, and, much upset and distressed, the king rose and walked out of the chamber, this in theory bringing the session to a close, although, in fact, the members continued with their contentious debating.

Thomas, moderate in matters of religion as he might be, was worried over this, foreseeing further troubles. He used his friendly relationship with Charles to urge a less literal attitude over this of divine right. But the other declared that this was something on which he could by no means yield. It was an integral part of kingship, and he was bound by his coronation oath – as indeed were those who had sworn fealty to him then. The late King James would almost certainly have adopted a less positive stance, in the cause of harmony, but Charles asserted that *he* could not, in all honesty. It was not a matter of personal choice and conviction but of God-given prerogative. However modest by nature, this monarch was not to be altered in his views on kingship.

Thomas remained worried, especially on account of the opposition already engendered by the English Puritans. Non-assertive by nature, Charles nevertheless looked like heading for conflict on this.

Whatever their differing views on divine right, the king demonstrated his continuing esteem and friendship with Thomas by appointing him Lord Advocate of Scotland. This was a highly important position. Not only did he advise and recommend on the appointment of high court judges, but of other law officers and officials. Charles again offered him a peerage, to be upsides with the new Earl of Haddington, Hamilton; but still he did not wish to have to spend overmuch time in London at the House of Lords. He gratefully declined. However, when the monarch suggested, in that case, converting his present status into one of the hereditary knighthoods created by the late King James, called baronetcies, he accepted that readily. So young Ian, who of course had been formally named John, would one day become Sir John Hope of Craighall.

To celebrate, Thomas bought the properties of Sandford and Balruddan. He had his eye on the fine estate of Luffness, at the head of Aberlady Bay over in Lothian, but he discovered that was not for sale, as it had just been purchased by, of all people, his rival, Hamilton, new Earl of Haddington. He was much put out over this.

14

Thomas did not greatly enjoy being Lord Advocate, for he found himself being approached by applicants anxious to be made judges, and sometimes these offered money to advance their cause, this needless to say much disapproved of. He guessed that Hamilton would have been similarly besought when occupying this position, and wondered whether he had succumbed to the temptation – which he dismissed from his mind as an unworthy speculation.

Very soon, in fact, he was faced with one of these situations. A Senator of the College of Justice, one Lord Kirkness, suddenly died, and had to be replaced. There was no lack of would-be substitutes. Which? How to choose? It was quite a serious responsibility, for the judge, whoever appointed, would have to decide on rights and wrongs and announce penalties, including that of death on occasion, a dire duty. It all led Thomas into much investigation and enquiries, this having to be done tactfully indeed. But *somebody* had to do it, and presumably he was considered to be fit for the task. Elizabeth declared that, judging by some of the appointments made to the bench recently, he was more worthy of the position than a few of his pre-decessors.

He had his first recommendation to make to the king quite soon, for the Lord Spottiswood of Newabbey was killed on being thrown from his horse at a hunt, and a successor was required. Enquiries led him to propose one,

Sir George Auchinleck of Balmanno, in Kincardineshire, of whom he had heard good reports as a commissioner for allocating those temporalities of the former Church lands, and not allowing pressure from acquisitive lairds and lords to affect his judgment – this appointment accepted by the monarch. Thomas felt the responsibility of nominating his first high court judge quite keenly.

Elizabeth meantime produced another child, their third daughter, whom they named Anne. Blessedly, she appeared to be healthy.

King Charles had not failed to learn of the income to be derived from walrus ivory, and kept in touch with Thomas on this matter. The parallel concern with Greenland, and co-operation with King Christian over the French Canadian situation, remained important, and Andrew Wood was kept active with his ships.

It was a matter other than ivory over which King Charles sent for Thomas for consultation. He had heard of the great survey made those years before, of all the former Church lands and their temporalities that had been appropriated by the Scots nobles at the Reformation. Now, religiously minded and concerned over worship, he had decided that these lands and their tithes should be bought back from the lairds and returned to the Church. He sought Thomas's help and guidance.

So, collecting all the many notes he had made and preserved of this major undertaking, he headed for London.

The king's proposal was that, using the Scots legal assumption that all the land was nominally the monarch's and bestowed by him into the care of his lordly subjects, he could revoke the royal grants made so long ago, and resume possession, paying the present holders for its current value. A due proportion of all this would be paid to the reformed Church, as compensation. The remainder would accrue to the nation's treasury. Would Thomas, as Lord Advocate as well as compiler of the survey, advise on this?

To say that that man was astonished at this project was to put it mildly. Had his Grace considered the cost? It would be enormous.

Would it not be but an exercise on paper? he was asked. The value of the land would still remain, possibly even increase, and the treasury would benefit in the end, as well as the Church.

Shaking his head, Thomas wondered whether Charles had any least notion as to the value of these vast lands, and the cost of buying them back from the present owners. It would be beyond all computation.

The king reiterated that it would be but figures on paper. The land would not lose its value. Wealth could be calculated in other than gold and silver.

But it was gold and silver that the lords and lairds would demand as payment, if by the royal prerogative they had to sell – and that itself was very doubtful, Thomas judged. In theory all the land might ultimately be the crown's, but not in fact. No court of law could force the owners to yield up property, at whatever price the crown was prepared to pay for it.

Charles was much crestfallen over this assertion by his Lord Advocate. He had been painting such a splendid picture of his northern kingdom's and Church's advance in credit and worth, and now it was dashed by his own legal adviser. But he held to the essence of it all. Since the crown was the ultimate and original holder of all the land of the realm, all grants of it could be revoked, surely. And if non-compliance with the royal command was demonstrated, the crown could indeed revoke such, and the property would return to the monarch.

Thomas declared that, although this *might* be so in theory – and he was uncertain as to that – in practice it was quite unachievable. The owners, or their predecessors, had bought these lands, and the crown had accepted and received its share of the payment. Nothing could alter that. No claim of royal reclamation would stand in law.

He could revoke the royal grant, Charles insisted, as still primary and ultimate owner. As monarch he could revoke any monarchial grant. Who was in a position to deny it?

If that was so, Thomas declared, due compensation could and would be demanded by the unwilling-to-sell owners, who could ask a price beyond all paying.

The crown could not be forced to pay any sum larger than the actual value of the land, Charles held.

Thomas wagged his head. This young king, so mild and hesitant in manner, was displaying a side to his character hitherto not evident. It was strange – and somewhat alarming as to future possibilities.

They left it at that.

There was another and awkward matter that had to be put to the monarch. This was the upset and apprehension in much of Presbyterian Scotland over Queen Henrietta Maria's strong holding to the Roman Catholic Church, and her constant display thereof; and to fears that she could well imbue her offspring with the like. This, and the fact that Charles himself was inclined towards bishops. The Church of Scotland was strongly Calvinist, and there were widespread fears over the situation, and the possibility that the monarchy might seek to impose episcopal supremacy on the northern kingdom. Bishops there still were, of course; but it would be a grave error to increase them and their authority, and to allow them back into seats in the Scottish parliament, as was being talked of. Charles, sighing, said that he would keep that in mind. Thomas could hardly add that the queen's influence in matters religious was to be guarded against.

He did urge Charles to pay a visit to Scotland soon, to greet, and display his pride, affection and esteem for, his northern subjects. This the monarch said that he would do.

Then Thomas was for home, with promises to consult further his notes on those thirteen hundred parishes, communities and estates of Scotland.

Elizabeth presented him with another son shortly thereafter, once again a sickly and feeble child, whom they named after the monarch. Sadly, he too died soon, as had those others. The couple decided that enough was enough. They had six children, after all. They were not going to risk any more births, four deaths sufficient. Their children were John, called Ian, Thomas called Tam or Tammy, Alexander, James, Mary and Anne.

Not only Thomas but most of Scotland was shocked when, shortly thereafter, the king issued a personal Act of Revocation. There were indeed doubts as to whether he had any royal right to do so, without parliamentary agreement. By it he announced that all holders of lands, including former Church ones, and the tithes thereof, required royal confirmation, under ancient and undeniable monarchial supremacy. These could be recovered by purchase from the king, at an agreed land-valuation price.

A great outcry was the immediate reaction, protest almost without exception from the landowning fraternity, from great nobles down to simple farmers, the Kirk's ministers included. The cost of such re-purchase from the crown, on a national scale, would be enormous, and all but impossible to calculate as well as to collect. Abruptly royal esteem and credit were shattered. That their seemingly kindly and benign monarch could so ordain was scarcely credible.

Thomas despatched an immediate letter to Whitehall urging a prompt revocation of this Act of Revocation. He added that to effect the policy was almost totally impossible, the very assessment of the charges being a huge task demanding long delay, and collecting the moneys from an outraged population unachievable.

The subsequent withdrawal of the Act of Revocation ordered by the two parliaments did not do the royal prestige any good. And the Duke of Buckingham, who was understood to have advised Charles on this folly, was impeached by the English parliament forthwith. He had the king then dissolve that parliament. But the damage was done. Never, possibly, had the crown's repute and esteem sunk so low.

Adding to this decline was the spectacular failure of an English expedition put forward with the intention of assailing the Spanish port of Cadiz, again at Buckingham's urging, as Lord High Admiral. This was so poorly organised and equipped that it never got as far as that destination, costly as it had been. Calls for the duke to be punished were vociferous; and to seem to meet the popular demand, Charles had his favourite appear before a sitting of the Star Chamber, an especial court of law called only by the monarch to enforce royal proclamations and edicts. This, needless to say, absolved Buckingham from any blame, and he walked free. But this development did King Charles's reputation no good. Thomas wished that, somehow, the duke could be got rid of. What with this favourite, his unpopular Catholic queen, and his weak hand on the tiller of state, Charles's reign was being less than successful. His father James, oddity as he was, had been a deal more effective.

Still Charles did not visit his northern realm and birthplace, despite Thomas's pleas.

In the autumn of 1627 the elderly Lord President of the Court of Session retired; recommending the appointment of a successor and of a new senator to complete the judiciary team was Thomas's duty, one of the innumerable such. This resulted in the situation where every one of the high court judges had been nominated by himself, a daunting thought. Had this ever happened before? He hoped that his nominees would all prove worthy. It was a responsibility that worried him sometimes. It meant, despite the lofty titles of some of the great nobles, Lord High Admiral, Lord High Justiciar, Lord High Chamberlain, Earl Marischal, Lord Lyon King of Arms and the rest, he, the Lord Advocate, was all but ruling Scotland in the monarch's absence, another daunting thought. He by no means sought all these responsibilities, but they came with the appointment. So more enquiries, considerations and judgment were called for. He came to the conclusion that Sir John Skene of Curriehill, a former Lord Clerk Register, should be nominated. At least *he* ought to be knowledgeable as to the duties, for his father had been in that position many years before.

There was now a problem before Thomas. That Act of Revocation had been unpopular enough to cause its abandonment, but some gesture was called for in the royal cause. He had sympathy with the king over this, and recognised his duty, not only as Lord Advocate but as a baron to his liege-lord, to serve him to the best of his ability, as sworn at his appointment. And this of extra royal dues, made evident by his survey some years before, could much add to the royal revenues. But he did not wish to offend the many owners of lands throughout Scotland who could be ordered to pay more; this would only make the governing of the realm more difficult, and probably defeat its own purpose. Some medium and moderate course was called for. Fortunately, with so many and widespread properties involved, only a token sum as gesture from each would nevertheless amount to a very sizeable total. But the collecting thereof would be in itself a major task. How was this to be achieved, and economically? Sending collectors in the king's name all around the country would be expensive, and scarcely worth while in view of the small amounts for each property. Would not some assembly of the lords, lairds and barony-holders be the answer, each bringing their lands' contributions with them? A parliament, then? There had not been one in Scotland for long, and such was overdue for other reasons than this. Would Charles come north for such? He had shown his reluctance to do so clearly enough in other respects. He was scarcely likely to do so as seeming just to collect moneys. So, a Lord Commissioner to represent him at a parliament? That would serve.

He wrote to Charles, suggesting the appointment of a Lord Commissioner to act for him at a parliament, the commissioners and representatives of the royal burghs commanded to bring their royal dues with them, to hand over for transmission to London. Small as these token sums were, there would be enough of them to reach a large amount. This seemed to be the advisable procedure.

The king was glad to agree.

*   *   *

After the necessary forty days' notice, the parliament duly assembled at Edinburgh Castle. A notably large attendance was achieved, for it had been long since such had been held, overlong in Thomas's opinion. The Chancellor, Hay of Kinfauns, Viscount Dupplin, although newly appointed, kept fair order – as was not always the case.

There was much procedural business, owing to the long period since the last assembly: appointments to be made and others confirmed, revenue statements to be given, the matter of the royal dues to be discussed, import and export taxes to be reviewed, and the like. Thomas had his statements to make regarding the monopolies situation, the French-Canadian position, and the Faroes leases, with their Danish connections, these as well as his usual Lord Advocate's reports, Elizabeth viewing all from the minstrels' gallery.

It was a less rowdy session than sometimes, although there was some heat generated over the revival of ancient royal dues for the monarch absent in England. The appointment of judges came up, and queries were asked as to certain nominees, which Thomas was able to answer with general acceptance.

Discussion kept coming back to the non-appearance of King Charles in his ancient realm: was this on account of his Catholic queen who might well see Calvinist Scotland as anathema? Thomas asserted that it was not. The young monarch had a great number of problems to face and decisions to take in the south, especially over French concerns, and those of Catholic–Protestant clashes in Ireland.

Considering all the other officers of state there present, Thomas felt that he was being overmuch called upon to answer for national affairs generally. Elizabeth could have reminded him that, by most present, he was seen to be all but ruling Scotland for Charles, which was not really the Lord Advocate's responsibility.

Parliament adjourned, and at the feasting that followed down at Holyrood, Thomas had some talk with three of the men whom he had advised the monarch to make Senators of the College of Justice and Lords of Session, these presumably grateful to him. Between them, they agreed that all high court procedures should be scrutinised, and where advisable amended, and certain anomalies adjusted. The next session of parliament would be asked to confirm this to ensure that justice was seen to be assured for all and not inclined towards the highly placed. Such measures were right and proper, but not apt to make the instigators more popular with the aristocracy, Elizabeth pointed out. Thomas declared that reform in matters religious had been effected; now were matters of the state and the law to be left unreformed?

The payment of those royal dues had been effected at the outgoing from the parliament. It amounted to slightly less than Thomas had calculated, although still a very rewarding total. So Scotland's contribution to the United Kingdom's finances would be creditable. It was to be hoped that England's would be commensurate, however assessed. Thomas could not make any real impact there, but at least the Scots had demonstrated the policy that could suitably be followed. He was reasonably optimistic.

Charles Stewart ought to be grateful.

15

The king, however, was less than joyful, for only a few weeks later, on 22 August, Buckingham was assassinated; and although Charles grieved sorely much of England rejoiced, for the duke had been notably unpopular, his behaviour arrogant, and his military gestures as ineffective as they were costly. In March the previous year an expedition organised and personally led by him, this to La Rochelle to aid the French Protestants, had been thoroughly defeated; and one of the participants, a naval lieutenant named John Felton, who had lost his brother in the action, stabbed the duke to death. *He* paid the price, although most saw the murder as a blessing.

Scotland was unconcerned, Thomas being one of the few in any way interested.

The matter of monopolies was again beginning to occupy his attention. At first these exclusive rights in trade and industry had been an encouragement for individuals and groups to advance their activities, to the general wellbeing, this in England as well as Scotland. But as time went on, some of these privileges had been apt to become oppressive and injurious, the holders thereof in a position to keep raising prices, owing to the lack of competition. In 1624 the London parliament had passed an Act, called the Statute of Monopolies, by which all such were declared null and void, and to be replaced, where suitable, by what were termed Letters Patent, this phrase deriving from the Latin *patens* meaning open, accessible. Actually these were the reverse of open, the Letters giving an exclusive right to produce and market certain goods and services. The Scottish parliament had not concerned itself with this; and as a result sundry producers, and not a few, came north to operate freely therefrom, and thus were able to offer lower prices than in the south, and win trade. There were strong objections to this from London, and demands that Scotland should prevent such competition. But it worked in favour of Scots. The Lord Advocate was brought into the dispute, and Thomas had to make a ruling, London insisting that since it was now a United Kingdom, the Scots must accept a similar legal stance.

He, after due enquiries, refused. The London parliament was in no position to dictate in this, as in other affairs. If English traders, merchants and producers found it profitable to act from Scotland, let them do so, and legally. No Statute of Monopolies had been enacted by the Scots parliament. As a result there was quite an influx of southerners over the border, and, better still, many Scots agents appointed to represent producers, this leading to an increase in trade. Here was one way of stealing a march on the Auld Enemy, to the enhancement of Thomas's popularity.

He was worried about King Charles. That monarch, now aged thirty, was acting up to his belief in the divine right of kings, however personally moderate and deeply religious. With a House of Commons largely dominated by Puritans, this was producing friction; and having a Catholic and strong-minded queen in Henrietta Maria did not help. The Commons produced a statement condemning what was called a revival of Popish practices, and blaming the king. Assured of his God-given right, Charles had ordered the adjournment of that parliament, and indicated that mean-time he was not going to call another. He added that he was, however, a loving and indulgent father to his people. This move distinctly alarmed Thomas and the Scots people, even though *their* parliament was not involved in this announcement.

This reign looked like being a troubled one.

At least, however, the succession was assured, for the queen gave birth to an heir, a healthy boy, who was called after his father: Charles, Prince of Wales and Duke of Rothesay.

Still the king did not make a return visit to Scotland, to Thomas's disappointment.

In these circumstances he had to make frequent journeys down to London, to gain authority for actions, have documents signed, and receive instructions from the mon-arch – although these last were apt to be but confirmations of his own plans and decisions, Charles being but little concerned with the Scottish situation. Thomas usually chose to go and return by ship, and this enabled Elizabeth on occasion to accompany him, to her pleasure and his – for she enjoyed excursions and visits to the court; and the young people were now of an age to be left on their own, at Craighall or Edinburgh's Cowgate.

Thomas gained an especial satisfaction that summer. He had, in such spare time as was accorded him, translated from the Latin the Psalms of David and the Song of Solomon, this in order that the ordinary Scots folk attend-ing divine worship should understand what was being said and sung. These were to be published in book form. And as well as this, something of less general interest but with its own value, a volume on the Process of Law, Scots law, and with the English equivalent in parenthesis as it were. Not a great many would find this of importance save other lawyers, but it might serve of use more generally in time to come. Could he now call himself an author?

That great survey of his, made all those years before, now proved of renewed value, for the Scots Privy Council, on which he sat, declared that a revised land-value register should be compiled, this to regularise taxation and improve the national revenues, ever a matter of concern. An investigating commission was to be set up, and, because of that survey, Thomas to chair it. He was well aware that, once again, this would not make him popular with landowners. But, after all, the land was ultimately the nation's wealth, and the holders thereof only trustees, even though they called themselves owners, this under the crown, the nation's representative. In England it was different, the owners outright proprietors. But in Scotland the crown, the people and the land formed a sort of triumvirate, and must remain so. Thomas felt strongly about this, and sought to demonstrate it personally in how he managed his own estates and treated his tenants. And he kept adding to his lands as his wealth increased. Elizabeth was amused by his attitude to land, asserting that he was land-hungry while claiming that the land was really the people's. Had he not just bought another large estate, that of Kingarroch and Batullie, there in Fife?

At any rate, the Land Register was drawn up, documented and established, with the royal dues declared, to Charles's satisfaction and financial assistance, making him the more grateful to Thomas.

So at last Charles was persuaded by his Lord Advocate to come to Scotland, after the long delay. And a great success the visit proved to be, the people eager to see and welcome their own Scots-born monarch. Great celebrations were organised, in especial a coronation ceremony at Holyrood, however belated, even though the king could not sit on the true Stone of Destiny, it being still hidden somewhere in the Hebrides. This solemnity drew some criticisms, however, because, at the crowning, he was anointed with oil, a usage that the Presbyterians disapproved of as Popish, as was the Episcopalian service held on the Sunday in St Giles High Kirk with the two clerics wearing white gowns instead of the preferred black. The palace of Holyroodhouse was hastily refurbished and smartened up, new tapestries hung on all the walls when it was discovered that the old ones had largely been eaten by rats. Arches of flowers and greenery were erected in the capital's streets, which were especially cleaned for the occasion, this necessary because of the female citizens' habit of flinging bucketfuls of dirty water from the tenement windows with warning shouts, to walkers and riders below, of "Gardyloo", meaning *guardez l'eau*. The heads of executed murderers and felons, normally exposed on spikes in prominent places, were removed, even tapestries hung on outer walls, and the great well at the Mercat Cross converted to spout wine instead of water, at which all might drink to the monarch's health.

Charles, much impressed by it all, declared that London had never been thus arrayed for him. Thomas had had his hand in the preparations.

Thereafter he accompanied, indeed conducted, the royal party on a tour of the land – or some of it, for Charles said that he could be away from London and affairs of state only for one month at the most. And Scotland, although with only one-tenth of the population of England, was over three-fifths the size, and with all its hills and mountains, lochs, passes and firths, was much more time-consuming to travel through, however much more dramatic and scenic. The Highlands and Isles, of course, could be given only a gesture at visiting; but the cities and larger towns were called at, although none north of Inverness, and areas such as Wester Ross, Skye, Mull, Kintyre, Arran and Galloway had to be bypassed. Glasgow, now become the largest of populations in the northern kingdom, laid on celebrations much to outdo Edinburgh's.

Charles enjoyed it all, knighted not a few, especially those who hosted him and his train overnight in their castles, and others whom Thomas suggested. It was long since a monarch had toured Scotland, for after James had gone to London he had only once returned to his original kingdom, and then for but a brief sojourn. Even so, the father's visit had generated more acclaim, for, while Charles was dignified and regal and James was anything but, ungainly and slovenly, he was apt to be boisterously good-humoured and accessible to his subjects.

Charles, on his departure, left a somewhat ominous intimation behind him. He declared that he would send north a Church Service Book, this to replace the Book of Common Prayer, commonly known as Knox's Liturgy, to be used in all parish churches. Not unnaturally this aroused much apprehension in Presbyterian Scotland, in view of the king's Episcopalian leanings. Thomas went so far as to advise otherwise, but was not heeded. What produced misgivings was the fact that it had been composed by Archbishop Laud of Canterbury, whose reputation in Scotland was low, however high church. Was Charles seeking to impose "Laud's Liturgy" instead of Knox's?

When the book did arrive it was greeted with anger and disdain. At the first reading, in St Giles High Kirk of Edinburgh by the dean, he was interrupted by loud cries from the congregation, these culminating in a stool being thrown at his pulpit by a woman named Jenny Geddes, who shouted, "Dost thou say Mass at my lug?" The service ended in riot, the Bishop of Edinburgh and other clerics being pelted with mud and rubbish by the mob when they escaped out into the street.

Thereafter only a very few parish ministers throughout the land dared to read from the book, despite the royal command. Charles's reputation and esteem suffered another blow.

Thomas shook his head over the monarch. The Book of Church Worship was rejected by Scotland. Sad it was, Thomas considered, that religion, the worship of the God of Love, so often produced animosity and hostility among mankind made in His image.

Charles was crestfallen, his aims no more successful in Presbyterian Scotland than in Puritan England.

Thomas sought to console and advise him. The Scots people would go their own way, in religion as in much else. Even the monarchy must recognise this. Let Charles send his good wishes to the forthcoming General Assembly of the Kirk of Scotland, in token, and indication that he was prepared to accept that the Book of Church Worship was not for them.

Depressed, the young king agreed. When was this Assembly? When he was told that it was in two months' time, he asked whether Thomas would be prepared to represent him thereat, as Lord High Commissioner. Such would not conflict with his duties as Lord Advocate, would it?

Thomas did not think that a Lord Advocate had ever before been Commissioner to the Assembly, but saw no reason why there should be any clashing of interests, although he much doubted that he would make a worthy occupant of that lofty office. Charles assured him that he would, and he would so appoint him.

So there was a deal of thought to be put into how he was to act, and what to say, at this assembly of Kirk ministers. He must remember that he would be there representing the monarch, not just himself, and so not to say anything that Charles would find reason to refute – which might be quite difficult. He scarcely looked forward to the occasion.

In due course it took place. Thomas was led in, with style and ceremony, to open the proceedings, but with hardly welcoming glowers from many of the delegates, the assumption being, no doubt, that he represented the monarchy's Episcopalianism. He was, needless to say, most careful as to his opening remarks, seeking to steer a non-controversial course, which in fact he felt was a pointless exercise and all but hypocritical since he had opinions of his own, and he represented the king there, who had such pronounced views in matters of religion.

Thomas quickly became aware that his care was not echoed by most of those present. The numbers were almost equally divided between what they termed the Moderates and the Evangelicals – and the former were by no means restricting themselves to moderation, nor were the Evangelicals. From the start it was a stormy session, with love and charity far from evident, efforts to have order prevail less than successful. More than once he felt like bringing proceedings to a close, but recognised that this was not his duty. Maintaining order was, though no easy task.

On only one issue was the Assembly united: this was in a rejection of Charles's, or really Archbishop Laud's, new prayer book. It was declared to be a work of the devil. Something being called a Covenant was called for. A committee was appointed to compose the wording of this, and not to delay about it. The actual wording might well be the cause of further dispute, but the demand for this National Covenant was all but unanimous. And King Charles was certainly going to condemn it. As his representative there Thomas had to tread warily indeed, whatever his own views.

He was thankful when he was able to close that Assembly. He would be much interested to see the final wording of the Covenant agreed upon – if actual agreement was ever reached.

The Scots, he judged, were the most argumentative race on God's earth.

Thomas hoped that he would not be the Lord High Commissioner at the next General Assembly of the Kirk, when this Covenant was presented for endorsement. That would be a notably controversial and noisy occasion.

That year Thomas, Earl of Haddington died – so *his* views on the wording of this Covenant document would not apply.

16

As Lord Advocate Thomas had to scrutinise the wording of
the Covenant in order to ensure that there were no *legal*
anomalies or inaccuracies, however many others there
might be. It was brought to him by James Graham, fifth
Earl of Montrose, a handsome young man who had been
prominent in demanding it and drawing it up. Thomas
found no fault in it, indeed agreed with its contents as well
as the wording.

They decided that a ceremonial public signing of support
for this so important document was called for, not just an
assembly of divines, or even a parliamentary endorsement. It
should be held in the capital, but probably not in St Giles High
Kirk, or Cathedral as the Episcopalians were now calling it.
So the church of Greyfriars, which stood somewhat to the
south, beyond the valley of the Grassmarket, was chosen.

There the great occasion took place, and great it was,
with literally thousands thronging to add their signatures to
this momentous document, not only the prominent and
influential; indeed there were far too many to do so in the
church itself, so much of the endorsement had to be done
on tombstones in the kirkyard outside. Montrose was the
first to sign.

It all represented a Scottish affirmation that Charles
could by no means ignore. Copies of this Covenant were
to be sent to all the parishes of the land in order that the
population as a whole should show its strong support.

The success of the Covenant-signing resulted in a national demand for a parliament to be called in the name of the people, not the monarch, this becoming a clamour. An especial Assembly of the Kirk was held in Glasgow, not in Edinburgh, the capital, for added significance, and this sat for an entire month in order to ensure that the Covenant's requirements were effected. It was to put an end to bishops, Laud's Liturgy, and to set up Presbyterianism as the accepted and official worship of Scotland.

Thomas wrote to Charles urging him to accept this declaration. There was little doubt that episcopacy had minimal support in the northern kingdom. The Kirk had the backing of the vast majority of the people. Let him give their worship his blessing.

But the king wrote back, saying that bishops had been God's appointed representatives under the monarchy since time was, and this of presbyters and so-called divines was error, wholly wrong. He, as the Lord's Anointed, had the simple duty of seeing that the true form of worship prevailed, in England against the Puritans and in Scotland against these unholy Presbyterians. And he would ensure it by royal decree and, if resisted, even by force of arms.

Appalled at this last, Thomas decided that he must go to London to try to persuade the monarch of the folly, indeed the sin, of seeking to impose episcopacy on the nation of Scotland.

Certain of his prearranged engagements of importance delayed his journey south, and when he was preparing to set out he learned that Charles had forestalled him, and had assembled a small army under some of his English nobles, and was in fact marching north to assert his authority. Equally alarmingly, Master Alexander Henderson, the stern Moderator of the General Assembly, and General

Alexander Leslie, a veteran commander of the German wars, had mustered a force to counter this royal threat, led by the King of Scots as it was.

It looked as though actual war loomed.

What could Thomas do to seek to prevent this? He was told that the king was already at Newcastle, and that Leslie's host had crossed Tweed just west of Berwick. Confrontation was near.

In haste Thomas rode south. He had no difficulty, at least, in locating the Scots force, for Leslie had been demanding reinforcements from the Border lairds, especially from the Homes, and all were able to tell of his whereabouts. He came to the Covenant array, about eight thousand strong, at the Birks, a location on the south side of Tweed three miles west of Berwick. With Charles marching from Newcastle the two armies were not far apart.

What should he do? Remain with Leslie in the hope that when the two hosts came face to face he could go forward and try to mediate, persuade Charles, if he could, to parley and treat rather than fight? Or seek out the king first, beforehand? The folly of it all!

He decided to approach the monarch. Once armies were on the move towards each other, and men prepared for battle, it could be more difficult to quell martial ardour. See Charles first, then.

He headed for Newcastle, with a couple of young Home lairds' sons, who knew the terrain, and how the king's host would be likely to advance.

With the guides, Thomas was able to reach the royal array, in the Fenwick area of Northumberland. Declaring to outriders that he was Scotland's Lord Advocate come to treat with the king, he was conducted to the presence. He judged this host a much larger one than Leslie's.

Charles greeted him kindly enough, in the company of the Percy, Earl of Northumberland and the Prince-Bishop of Durham, with sundry local lords. But when he heard Thomas urging an acceptance of the Covenant and Presbyterianism, he waved a royal hand in refusal. That document was all but a denial of his monarchial authority, he declared, and as such had to be suppressed, and forthwith. He was not going to treat with its supporters.

However, the Percy, with the Nevilles, Radcliffes, Umfravilles and Ridleys, lords of these parts, were less eager. All were much aware of the dangers of cross-border fighting, and its ongoing repercussions. They almost all sided with Thomas in advising negotiation rather than battle. And however reluctantly, Charles had to agree – so long as that wretched creature Henderson, the so-called Moderator, was not one of those he had to deal with. Thomas, with the Graham Earl of Montrose, offered to act as go-betweens.

The pair rode northwards to the neighbourhood of Duns, in the Merse, where, under a bed-sheet serving as a white flag, they were conducted to a great encampment, where the leaders' tents were hung with blue and white banners bearing the statement, "For Christ's Crown and Covenant".

However, they found the Covenant leaders little more eager for civil war than were Charles's supporters. The basis of some sort of treaty was concluded between the sides, whereby another General Assembly and a parliament meeting were to be held at Edinburgh, simultaneously, and the overall situation debated with a view to a settlement acceptable to both parties. Charles was distinctly doubtful about this, as seeming to lessen his divine authority. But Thomas's and Leslie's advice prevailed, in what became known as the Pacification of Berwick – even though few involved saw this as really marking an end to the struggle between king and Covenant. Charles was only persuaded to accept its terms on account of the problems arising out of his disagreement with the *English* parliament, largely Puritans, which was refusing to allot him money to pay the lords for the recruitment of men to make up the necessarily large army. There was even talk of mutiny in his present array, among the rank and file over non-payment of wages. Seldom, surely, had a king been so out of step with his subjects both north and south of the border. The disgruntled monarch returned to London to try to persuade parliament there to support him, leaving his army at Newcastle.

He was unsuccessful in this, finding its members almost solidly against him.

Thomas wrote to him there, saying that if he publicly accepted and endorsed the Covenant, and promised no advancement of episcopacy, the Scots, basically loyal, would espouse his cause.

The unfortunate king, faced with hostility in England, went through the motions of appearing to approve of the Covenant, however little that was true, and did come north again to Scotland, Thomas and Montrose meeting him at the border.

The royal reception at Edinburgh was markedly different from that of seven years before. Then he had been welcomed by a cheering population in the streets; now nothing such, only formal ceremonial by the magistrates and certain of the nobility, no crowds. Such banqueting as was provided at Holyrood had to be at his own expense, with only a modest attendance of great ones. He sought to win some popular credit by creating two well-thought-of nobles, Campbell, Earl of Argyll, and Graham, Earl of Montrose, marquises, but that did not greatly interest the people at large. Thomas was offered a peerage again, but once more respectfully declined on account of the duties involved at the House of Lords. The visit to the northern kingdom was not a resounding success. Charles Stewart was an unfortunate monarch, handsome and seemingly amiable as he might be.

Thomas obtained one satisfaction over this royal visit. It was the Lord Advocate's privilege to advise the king on appointments of judges for the high court. Thomas's sons John, Thomas, Alexander and James were all lawyers of ability and Charles, meeting the eldest son, John, whom Thomas and Elizabeth always called Ian, promptly knighted him. In addition he suggested that the father should recommend the son to him to be a Lord of Session. Doubtful as he was about the wisdom of this, and the reception by the legal fraternity, but urged on by Elizabeth, John became Lord Craighall of Session.

The appointment gave rise to an interesting development, quite apart from the administration of justice. It had always been the custom in the high court of Scotland that all must bow and take their hats off to the presiding judge, this including the Lord Advocate. But it was considered unsuitable that a father should have to doff his bonnet to his son, and it was made a rule that the Lord Advocate need not do so hereafter but might keep his head covered in court.

And shortly thereafter, too, came a further mark of esteem towards Thomas's family when his youngest son James was appointed Master of the Mint.

Meantime the extraordinary situation continued of two armies facing each other, not far apart on either side of the border, neither with any desire to assail the other, indeed with a certain amount of intercommunication, the English one in some disarray, something like rebellion simmering in the ranks on account of non-payment for the men. One small engagement did take place when parties of outriders encountered each other up-Tweed, and the smaller English group had to turn tail. It was all quite ridiculous in a united kingdom, with the monarch away seeking funds from his hostile southern parliament.

He did not get them. Seething with discontent, the English army turned back from Newcastle and marched off southwards, dispersing as it went. The Scots force could do the same. Nobody was quite sure whether they were at war or not.

An especial sitting of the Scots parliament was called, dispensing again with the required forty days' notice, at which the Lord Advocate assured that there was no reason for hostility with England, only the monarch's demands in dispute. Charles was insisting on restoring episcopacy in Scotland, but was in no position to enforce it, his English Puritan-dominated parliament far from supporting him. Let peace prevail.

But peace was easier to hope and pray for than to establish, and this in both realms. The English parliament re-established itself without royal authority, and, Puritan and almost consistently anti-Charles, demanded sweeping changes. And in Scotland, although the king had been persuaded to agree to the Covenant, the Covenanters themselves had split into two opposing groups, the extremists very aggressive, this of Charles wishing to restore bishops to power in the Church known and to be contested. A party was even demanding that Charles should abdicate and his twelve-year-old son son ascend the throne as Charles the Second; and this attitude was reflected by a section of the Puritans in England.

Such assault on the royal authority aroused indignation in many in the northern kingdom, as well as in England, and a movement was initiated to support the monarch. Prominent in this was the new Marquis of Montrose, despite the fact that *his* signature had been the first on the Covenant. No disloyalty to the crown had been behind that document, only concern over the feared imposition of the rule of bishops in the Kirk. Now the marquis led the proceedings to uphold the monarchy. A new assertion was drawn up and distributed, entitled the Solemn League and Covenant, this to pledge assistance to the moderates in the English parliament on condition that the Church there would be reformed, this opposed by the extreme Puritans.

Once again, religion seemed to be instigating clash instead of divine love. Thomas, for one, sought to play this down.

Thomas Wentworth, Earl of Strafford, a leading adviser of Charles, former Lord Deputy of Ireland, and still a strong supporter, leading the anti-Puritans, was impeached by that parliament, imprisoned and executed, the extreme Presbyterians in Scotland applauding.

Thereafter what amounted to civil war broke out in England, those supporting the monarchy and the bishops against the Puritans. These last quickly produced an able commander in the field, an experienced soldier, son of a Huntingdon squire, named Oliver Cromwell who demonstrated expertise at the first and inconclusive Battle of Edgehill in that warfare. Thomas was much concerned that this battling did not spread to Scotland. Could he do anything to prevent it?

He went to see the Graham Marquis of Montrose, very much a king's man and a most competent envoy, seeking his co-operation to ensure peace in Scotland. Would this

Cromwell, if he succeeded in gaining Puritan control militarily in England, attempt to move over the border and try to dominate Scotland also?

Montrose hoped not; but recognised that the extreme Presbyterians might, in that case, invite him to do so. They must be prepared for this. Although military matters were not really the concern of the Lord Advocate, he besought the marquis, possibly in co-operation with Argyll, to ensure that sufficient strength was mustered so that the King of *Scots*' cause would not suffer. Montrose was glad to agree. He would see Argyll.

Storm clouds thickened over the two realms.

17

Quite quickly thereafter those storm clouds built up into actual warfare, civil war. King Charles, no military leader himself, put his loyalist forces under the command of his nephew, Prince Rupert, known as Rupert of the Rhine because of his cavalry successes in the Palatinate, a brilliant tactician. Rupert was the son of Charles's sister, the Princess Elizabeth, who had married Frederick the Fifth, Elector Palatine and King of Bohemia. He had won martial fame in the German wars, and had come to England to aid his uncle. Now he demonstrated his abilities, leading the royalists to victory first at Bristol, then relieving besieged Newark in Nottinghamshire, and going on to seize most of Lancashire. All seemed to be going well for the monarch, until that Oliver Cromwell who had won the Battle of Edgehill was put in command of all the parliamentary forces as captain-general, and fairly promptly thereafter was able to defeat Rupert at Marston Moor, in Yorkshire. Jealousy at Rupert's elevation by Charles to be Duke of Cumberland and Earl of Holderness, on the part of some of the English royalist leaders, especially John Digby, Earl of Bristol, divided the royal cause, and Cromwell took fullest advantage of this, and was able to defeat Rupert again at Naseby; whereafter that prince was relieved of his command, despite capturing Leicester, and reduced to captaining shipping for naval warfare. It proved to be a sorry loss for Charles.

In Scotland Montrose and Argyll sought to maintain the king's authority militarily, Thomas strong for him on the civil side, urging parliamentary support. But all were aware that if Cromwell brought his large and victorious army north – Roundheads as they were called, this because of the close-cropped hair they adopted – it would be difficult indeed to defeat him.

The king fled, and not to Scotland but to the Isle of Wight, which by no means helped his cause.

Cromwell finally defeated the Earl of Bristol and his colleagues in a series of battles in Lancashire. England was his. He proceeded to march into Scotland.

Unfortunately for Charles, and for Scotland itself, MacCailean Mor, as he was styled in the Gaelic, the Campbell Marquis of Argyll, decided that Cromwell was too strong to oppose successfully. He renounced his support for the king, and retired to his West Highland fastnesses. His fellow-marquis, Montrose, was left with General Alexander Leslie to command the opposition in the field, while Thomas sought to take the lead for the king in civil affairs.

This was none so easy, with Charles's folly in retiring to the Isle of Wight adding to his other failures, and with Argyll's departure into isolation. Presbyterian Scots were anything but enthusiastic over the now absent monarch's episcopal plans, with the threat of Cromwell ever present. Would it be wise to accept the last, welcome Cromwell's activities, at least meantime, avoiding conflict, even if that seemed a feeble stance for a proud nation? Montrose thought otherwise.

A Scots parliament sitting was assuredly called for; but clearly the king was not likely to summon one; and without the royal authority the Privy Council could only call a convention. But even that would be better than nothing. A Privy Council meeting, then?

Thomas approached Montrose, who agreed that this would be a wise step. But who had authority to call a council meeting? Thomas and Montrose were both counsellors. Argyll was one also, of course, but he appeared to be washing his hands as to national affairs. Who else? Probably a Lord Advocate and one marquis had never before sought to summon a Privy Council meeting. Some members might well refuse to attend, in the circumstances. But they could attempt it, especially if James, the new Duke of Lennox and far-out kinsman of the monarch, would agree to add his name.

He did, and in the event, given the forty days' notice, similar to that for a parliament, quite a representative turnout was achieved.

Although Lennox presided, Thomas really conducted the meeting. The counsellors were all but unanimous in their condemnation of the monarch's dereliction of his royal duties, and there were more suggestions that he should be advised to abdicate, and his fourteen-year-old son become Charles the Second, and come back from France where he lived with his mother and younger brother James. But reaching him and convincing him and his mother, Henrietta Maria, to do so would take time, and with Cromwell on the move north, time was in short supply. Surely Lennox's name and standing would be sufficient authority, with that of the Lord Advocate and the Marquis of Montrose?

But meantime, Cromwell! All recognised that to muster a sufficiently strong army to face and challenge that experienced commander, in time, was impossible. But the land itself? Scotland, especially north of the Forth and Clyde, was a terrain that could be used to help its own defenders, and one to which Cromwell was unused: unending hills and mountains, rivers and firths and lochs, undrained marshland, ravines and high passes, all this, and Highland clansmen in especial who knew how to use it to good effect, as did Montrose. But sadly the Scots were, as so often, divided, for and against the king, for and against competing forms of worship. The Highlanders were still largely Catholic and scorned the Lowlanders, especially the Covenanters and Presbyterians, and declared that they would bring over hordes of their Irish co-religionists to aid in the king's cause against both the English and the Calvinists.

With this situation Montrose, Thomas and Leslie had to cope. Their strategy was to lure Cromwell north into Perthshire and beyond, where his cavalry would be at major disadvantage amid the mountainous territory.

The marquis used the time-honoured method of rousing the Highlanders by sending out the Fiery Cross, this two pieces of stick tied crosswise, the ends burned and blackened and spread with goat's blood. Why this, nobody knew. These crosses were given to clansmen, who ran with them throughout the Highlands far and wide. On the chiefs' orders and thus stirred, all but the whole of the north rose to arms, and Montrose was able to persuade large numbers of Irish gallowglasses, as they were called, to come over and join his army. At the head of this array, he marched south.

Thomas awaited him at Edinburgh.

At Tippermuir, near Perth, Montrose won a swift and resounding victory, this in no more than ten minutes, with the Covenanters ill-led and mainly less than able fighters. Then he headed back north-east for Aberdeen, which he took; but there was himself distressed by the behaviour of his troops, the Irish in especial, who, looking on the population as godless recusants, robbed, plundered and slew, even making their prisoners, men, women and children, take off their clothes before they killed them, so that these would not be spoiled by blood. In vain Montrose sought to tame and discipline these supporters.

Partly as a result of this conduct, and the losses incurred by some of his own Campbell clan, and partly through jealousy of his co-marquis's military successes, Argyll at last emerged from his fastnesses and took the field, this not exactly pro-Covenant but anti-Montrose. A great battle was fought at Inverlochy, below the great mountain of Ben Nevis, which Montrose won. Argyll retired again, to lick his wounds.

The Covenanters found a new general, called Baillie, who sought to discipline that faction, as Montrose was doing with *his* supporters, but with scant success also. At Kilsyth, between Stirling and Glasgow, that August of 1645, the two armies met, the Covenant and Argyll's force almost double the size of Montrose's. But superior leadership, together with quarrelling between the Campbell chief and Baillie, gave the victory to Montrose; this struggle became known as the Battle of the Shirts, because so hot was the weather that the royalists, on Montrose's orders, fought half naked. Making use of the terrain, as usual, especially a great marsh called the Dullatur Bog, he defeated Baillie and Argyll's force with major slaughter, only eight of Montrose's people being slain.

So now, with most of Scotland in his hands, including Glasgow and Edinburgh which Thomas was all but controlling in the king's name, Montrose had the upper hand, for Cromwell had been recalled to London to become the first chairman of the newly established Council of State, this in essence making England a republic. Meanwhile much of his New Model Army, as it was being termed, sat idle at Perth.

About this time Thomas had a vivid and unusual dream. He had had a fall from his horse some weeks before, which left him with a damaged ankle, and Elizabeth had presented him with a fine walking-stick with a silver handle. In his dream, he stumbled, and the stick broke in pieces, unlikely as this was. Strangely, the next night he had the same dream, with the stick again broken. He was not a great dreamer, nor apt to take dreams seriously; but to have such an odd vision twice, and so vividly, struck him as just possibly significant. Was this a warning of some sort?

He told Elizabeth of it, and she said not to be foolish. It was a good, sound stick of ash, and highly unlikely to break.

Nevertheless, Thomas wondered. And when, a few nights later, he had the same dream, the stick snapping and leaving him with the silver handle in his grip, he rather got the matter on his mind. That broken stick could signify the end of some progress, some journeying? But, left with the silver handle? Could that mean that the worth of it, the silver, remained with him? Progressing. Value? Value of what? His life? Hitherto, but progressing? A further life? He was very much a believer in the afterlife. Could this be an intimation to him that the progress thitherto was near?

He did not speak of it to Elizabeth again. But he was impressed enough, perhaps foolishly, to add a sentence at the end of the will that he had made up some time before, declaring that, in the event of his death, which must come one day, he wished to be buried without ceremony, and that his bones should be laid deep in the kirkyard of Greyfriars, in Edinburgh, where he had accompanied the great Montrose to sign the Covenant, not at the burial-ground of the parish church at Craighall, where they had interred their children who had died young. Was this a foolish whim? And all because of dreams.

That silver handle! Was that his assurance, his comfort? A pat on his back? That he had done none so badly, had made something of a mark, had achieved something in life? Of benefit to Scotland, and England also. Had served his king. His wife taking her place at court. He had advanced his offspring, his sons knighted, one Cup-Bearer to the king, two others being now Lords of Session, one daughter married to the Lord Cardross, the other to a son of the Earl of Mar. None so ill for a merchant's son, raised in the Cowgate of Edinburgh. He was now in his sixty-seventh year, and might live longer yet, despite that broken stick!

As it transpired, Thomas Hope did not. He died in 1646 of a heart attack, suffering no lengthy decline, and despite his will urging otherwise, was buried at Greyfriars, yes, but with great ceremony, the funeral attended by the highest in the land.

His tombstone was carved with the motto of the coat of arms that Charles had ordered the Lord Lyon King of Arms to grant him, "*At Spes Infracta*", meaning, "whatever else may perish, hope will not".

Epilogue

Scotland still had its worries and Montrose was faced with a vital problem. Should he attempt to assail this force at Perth, under its major-general deputising for Cromwell? That, in effect, would be to declare war on England in present circumstances. And those troops were notable and experienced soldiers, even if not at the guerrilla warfare at which he himself had become so expert. Best probably to leave them there meantime, in the hope that Cromwell would remain involved in his new Council of State and parliamentary situation, and this force remain more or less inactive.

Deciding that this was the right course, and with Thomas's son, James's agreement, that young man now giving aid and advice where possible, he went on with his campaign to control Scotland for the absent monarch.

He was much aided in this by an unexpected development. Ireland, or at least its great Catholic majority, saw the opportunity, with civil war in England and Scotland, to cast off its allegiance to the English crown. Many of its earls and lords, encouraged by the Catholic Church hierarchy, rose in arms and expelled the English keepers from towns and castles. And Cromwell, seeing this as grievous insurrection, judged the Irish situation much more urgent than the Scottish one, and embarked his New Model Army for Ireland.

The Scots heaved sighs of relief, James and Montrose

included. The gallowlasses returned to their own land. For the time being, Cromwell could not be forgotten, but relegated to the background.

However, the word came from England that he was not wholly preoccupied with this Irish campaign. King Charles was apprehended on the Isle of Wight and confined in its Carisbrooke Castle, charged, of all things, with high treason against his own realm, this by parliament and the Lord Protector. Could a king be charged with treason in his own kingdom? Only if *parliament* was supreme, in the name of the people, as the Lord Protector claimed.

There was no delay in proving this. A High Court of Justice was set up and the monarch brought to trial, declared guilty, and Cromwell, coming back for this, ordered the due penalty for treason – execution. He personally signed the death-warrant.

Poor Charles Stewart. Unwise he might have been, but scarcely deserving of this fate, a king to be executed by his own subjects. His grandmother, Mary, Queen of Scots, had died on the scaffold – but that was on the orders of her captor, Queen Elizabeth Tudor of England.

Scotland was shocked, if England was not.

Charles died bravely.

And the succession? He left two sons and a daughter, Charles, James and Mary. The eighteen-year-old youth was immediately proclaimed King Charles the Second by the Scots. This Cromwell's English parliament refused to do likewise.

So there was little of a United Kingdom left. And Ireland was in revolt. Young Charles might have been acknowledged as King of Scots, but that carried little weight with Cromwell and the English parliament. He was living in exile at The Hague. Would he deem it worth while to accept the challenge and come to his northern kingdom? Either to reign there at least, or, better, to seek to retake England from Cromwell? It was a vast task to put before the teenage Stewart. But Montrose and James Hope, along with many Scots lords, churchmen and leaders of the people, urged it. Come, Charles! Come, accepting the Solemn League and Covenant. Come, and act the king!

Montrose was deputed to go to the Netherlands, convince young Charles, and if possible bring him back.

In the Wassenaar Hof at The Hague, the Netherlands palace of Elizabeth, Queen of Bohemia and wife of the Elector Palatine, sister of the late King Charles and aunt of the new monarch, Montrose and James faced Sir Edward Hyde, principal adviser and fellow-exile of their young liege-lord, former Chancellor of the empty Exchequer, a plump, clever little man, son of a mere country squire, who had risen high in affairs of state.

"Sir Edward, King Charles should most certainly come to Scotland, where he is assured of the warmest and most loyal welcome. Let him act the King of Scots," James said. "He will rally the land against Cromwell, who is presently in Ireland. The people will flock to his standard, and encourage his many supporters in England to rise in arms for the crown. Cromwell, by his harsh rule, has lost the backing and esteem of most there. My lord Marquis, here, will the more successfully lead the English to emulate the Scots to fight in the royal cause if His Grace is there in Scotland rather than biding here in the Netherlands. You must see it."

"I see danger for His Majesty, my lords. They slew his father. They will slay *him* if they can. The man Cromwell would almost certainly come back from Ireland to lead against him and your Scots. You and your people carry your victories down into England *first*, so that it is safe for His Majesty to return."

"That would be infinitely more possible if His Grace was there, behind us." That was Montrose. "Seen to be leading the regaining of his throne . . ."

The door of the chamber burst open and a young man entered all but at the run. He was tall, slender, great-eyed, but sallow-complexioned and gangling as had been his grandfather, James the Sixth and First, for this was Charles Stewart, deep-breathing, as he had obviously just run up the stairs.

"I heard that you were here, Montrose himself!" he exclaimed. "They told me . . ." He stopped and shook his dark head, presumably recollecting his royal status. "I, I salute you, my great captain-general! I do, I do! And, and you, sir – you will be Sir James Hope, son of the Lord Advocate of Scotland, who has recently died."

"Yes, Sire – your most humble servant."

"Myself also, Your Grace." Montrose bent to reach for and take the royal hand between his own two palms in the traditional gesture of homage, bowing.

This Charles was unlike his father in almost all respects, far from handsome and dignified, but impulsive, eager. Not in the least religious, so unlikely to arouse controversy in that sphere.

James lost no time in declaring that he and the marquis had been urging that His Grace would be well advised to come back to Scotland with them, probably landing in the Orkneys and then heading southwards, acting the King of Scots and commanding his loyal Scots people to rise in his cause against Cromwell. He was interrupted by Hyde, who said that this would be dangerous folly, and that demonstration must first be made by the Scottish people that they were prepared to rise in their full strength to fight for him before he set foot on the land.

Montrose could also interrupt, and did so. He said that the king's presence would be highly important for the success of the proposed campaign, although he need not act in the field. But he should be *there*, not here waiting in the Netherlands.

It was at this stage that a newcomer entered the chamber, another Scots exile, John Maitland of Lethington, second Earl of Lauderdale, a man of thirty, tall and distinguished-looking, giving the impression of ability. His father had been President of the Scots Council and an Extra Lord of Session, created earl in 1624 and had died in 1645. The son had thrown in his lot with young Charles.

Hyde promptly told him that these two fellow-countrymen were urging the king to go back with them to Scotland in order to lead in the fight against Cromwell, the which *he* strongly contested as ill-advised and highly dangerous. If the villainous Cromwell returned from Ireland, as he almost certainly would, and triumphed in his warfare as he had so successfully done hitherto, then His Majesty's life would be at dire risk. Cromwell had, after all, had the king's royal father executed.

Lauderdale nodded and said that he agreed. It would be foolish to endanger His Grace thus. Here at The Hague he was safe, and he must remain safe. His presence in Scotland at this stage was not really necessary for the cause. But the cause itself was vital. He himself would be glad to go with the marquis and James to Scotland, but the king should remain here meantime.

James intervened. "I think that His Grace should indeed come to Scotland, and soon. But not forthwith. Let my lord

Marquis land first, in the north, muster a force and march south, to demonstrate resolute action. If, as it is to be hoped, and as I believe will happen, the folk rise in acclaim, *then* His Grace to come, to forward all."

"I agree," Lauderdale said. "Not go just yet, Sire. This would make you all but a fugitive in your own land. A lack of dignity. But if my lord Marquis gains a victory, then come, to be at the captain-general's back."

"That would be wise," James agreed. And added, "This of the Covenant, Sire. Not that Solemn League, shame on it, but the first and true Covenant. If Your Grace was to announce your royal support for that, it would, I say, greatly help, strengthening your cause with the people."

"Yes, indeed." That was Lauderdale.

Charles frowned. He misliked the original Covenant, if not as grievously as he did the second one, since it held the Presbyterian form of worship to be that of the Church of Scotland, not the Episcopalian. But he saw the practicality of agreeing to it, if it was what the Scots wanted, since he was by no means intensely religious.

"If this is needed, then I would accept it," he said, shrugging, after a momentary pause.

Hyde shook his head but did not speak.

Montrose looked at James. "That is well. I will go to Scotland. Land at Orkney, if that is advisable, then seek to raise a force to forward the royal cause. When, God willing, I have gained a sufficiency of the land, with the people backing us, and have taught these Covenanting Leslies their lesson, then His Grace should come over and make Scotland his. And pray that England will see its duty and do likewise. Get rid of Cromwell."

"That will be none so easy," Lauderdale warned.

"Ease, my lord, is not my motto! I prefer endeavour!"

"How? Where will you start?" Charles asked.

"At Orkney I ought to learn just what the situation is. Where Cromwell is now, and the Covenanting Leslies. Whether Argyll will be prepared to help. Decide on my course."

"I will come with you, there," James said. "It may be that I can assist, with fair knowledge as to who can be trusted to aid us. The Highland chiefs and their clans are still mainly Catholic, and loyal. They will rally to your banner, or His Grace's."

"If I come with you also, would that not be of help?" the king asked. "I would wish to."

All four of his hearers combined in advising not. Later, yes – but not until a campaign had started and some progress made. It would inevitably take time to rally the clans and loyal supporters further south; and meantime Cromwell could seek to capture and execute the king. Wait here, in The Hague, until Scotland was roused.

Reluctantly Charles acceded.

His three Scots advisers had to find a shipmaster to take them up to the Orkney Isles.

Was Cromwell still in Ireland?

At Kirkwall in Orkney they learned sad news. There had been a rally of the Covenant faction under its general, David Leslie, nephew of the now old Alexander Leslie, a veteran soldier. The Covenanters had marched to Perth and assailed that section of Cromwell's army left there, and gained a modified victory. This had brought the Lord Protector hastening back from Ireland, and taking vehement command, threatening dire vengeance. He was now indeed in stern mood, and Scotland was going to suffer.

So Montrose had two foes to fight, Cromwell's Ironsides

and the Covenanters under David Leslie. Why were the Scots always so divided against each other?

James and Lauderdale set out for the south, to do what they could to rouse the Lowland loyalists, leaving Montrose to muster the northern clans.

At Edinburgh, James learned grim tidings. Cromwell had met and defeated Leslie's Covenant army none so far off, at Dunbar in Haddingtonshire. Finding himself in a difficult position, in stormy weather with shipping not able to land food for his army, and the local people wasting the land before him, Cromwell had been making for the border. And had reached the Doon Hill not far from that town. What followed was a disaster indeed, but for Scotland not Cromwell. General Leslie had held a strong position on this hill. But egged on by the many divines and clergy with his host, the Covenanting troops ignored their general and rushed downhill, as their ancesters had done centuries before against English Edward the First, to get at the foe – and with the same result. Cromwell had been able to overwhelm them all completely with his disciplined array. His Ironsides, divided into two sections, had outmanoeuvred the Scots, front and rear. They had slain three thousand, and taken ten thousand prisoners, at a loss of only a score of his seasoned soldiers, driving the hordes of enthusiastic but unruly Scots before them like a great herd of cattle to the slaughter; indeed the catastrophe was being spoken of as the Dunbar Drove.

So much for patriotic flourish and religious fervour in the face of firm discipline and central command by an experienced general.

James was not long in learning further devastating news. From Orkney Montrose had sailed to near John o' Groats in Caithness, with about one thousand men, and then marched west to Thurso, on learning that Major-General Strachan, a Covenant leader, was at Tain on the Dornoch Firth in Easter Ross. At Thurso, near the very northern tip of mainland Scotland, the marquis raised the royal standard, calling on all loyal men to flock to it. No great numbers of Mackays, Mackenzies and MacLeods did so; and they had then been confronted by Strachan at Carbisdale, on the south side of the Kyle of Sutherland and, vastly outnumbered by the Covenanters, defeated and scattered. Montrose had escaped capture, and become a fugitive in that wild country. With the Earl of Kinnoull he had got as far as Loch Assynt, none so far from the west coast, where, finding Ardvreck Castle, a smallish tower-house belonging to Macleod of Assynt who had fought in the royal cause in the past, he had taken refuge therein. And Macleod had brought disgrace on the name of that clan, betraying the marquis and earl by sending for Major-General Holbourn, Strachan's second-in-command at Lochinver, and delivering his guests into that man's hands. Montrose was now a captive and held secure.

These dire tidings were followed by the arrival in Edinburgh of the notable prisoner himself, to be confined in the Tolbooth gaol. James sought to act on behalf of the king's captain-general, but he was promptly disclaimed by the Chancellor, the Campbell Earl of Loudoun, at the urgings of his chief, Archibald Campbell, Marquis of Argyll, MacCailean Mor, who had always envied and hated his fellow-marquis.

A farce of a trial followed, under Archibald Johnston, Lord Warriston of Session, and Montrose was found guilty of treason and condemned. He claimed that he had always acted with the king's authority as his captain-general, but this was dismissed as outdated and revoked. He was ordered to kneel, to hear his sentence. He refused to do so, saying that he only knelt to his God. He was kicked behind the knees to bring him down, and thus held.

The sentence, prepared in advance, was read out. It was to be hanging, beheading, quartering and displaying, this without Christian burial, and to take place the next day at two o'clock of the afternoon.

There was nothing that James could do to save the man he so greatly admired. All the power presently controlling Scotland was against him.

Montrose spent his last night, before he slept, composing two verses. One read:

Lord, since Thou knowest where all these atoms are,
I'm hopeful Thou'llt recover once my dust,
And confident Thou'llt raise me with the just.

And

He either fears his fate too much,
Or his deserts are small,
That dares not put it to the touch,
To gain or lose it all.

So, next day as he was led out to the scaffold, he produced a comb from his pocket, and used it to restore his fine, long, dark, wavy hair to neatness.

Warriston declared, "Man, in your state you would be better taking care of your immortal soul than for just your worthless body and appearance, combing your head!"

Montrose answered, "My lord, my head is still mine own. When it shall be yours, treat it as you will!" And he continued to comb.

He climbed the scaffold platform, to eye the thirty-foot-high gibbet, hands pinioned. Turning to the executioner, he smiled. "Now, my friend, play you your part. My hands are tied – but you will find some small moneys in my pocket."

Blinking and shaking his head, that man placed the noose round the victim's neck.

"God have mercy on this afflicted land!" he said.

So died James Graham.

It was mid-June as the great crowd waited near the jetty of the fishing-village of Garmouth, on Spey Bay, midway between Aberdeen and Inverness, watching the single vessel flying the Dutch flag as it approached the haven, many of the most prominent men in Scotland among them. It was perhaps scarcely a suitable location for the arrival of the King of Scots – who was also, of course, King of England – coming from The Hague to the northern kingdom, and only on a merchant ship. But that was the situation this June, one month after the execution of Montrose. And Charles, aged twenty, was going to have an equally strange reception indubitably, with the mass of divines already chanting, "Take the Covenant! Take the Covenant!"

James sympathised with his young liege-lord.

As the craft drew in, to moor at the wharf among the fishing-boats, William Keith, the Earl Marischal, flanked by Archibald Campbell, Marquis of Argyll, and another Campbell, the Chancellor, Earl of Loudoun, moved forward to await the running-out of a gangplank from the vessel. And still the chorus of "Take the Covenant" rang out. Indeed the clergymen moved forward also.

Frowning, the Marischal turned to the divine nearest him. "Master Cant, wait you," he ordered. "It is my simple duty to receive His Grace first, lacking the presence of his lieutenant-governor and viceroy." That was an oblique reference to the late Montrose. "Then you and yours may have your say."

"I say that this is Christ's kingdom before it is Charles Stewart's!" he was told. "As such he must have reception. You, my lord, represent the second, we the first!" Still the chanting persisted.

"The Kirk takes precedence," another cleric asserted. That was the Reverend Robert Blair, from Aberdeen. "You, sirrah, are but an earthly vassal of an earthly monarch. We speak in the name of the Most High!"

"Indeed? Who made you so?"

It was from behind the Marischal that there was intervention, and in a quietly sibilant Highland voice, but positive enough to be heeded, even by divines, for this was MacCailean Mor himself, the Marquis of Argyll, he with a notable cast in one eye, and foxy, narrow-chinned features. "Wait you," he advised – and it was difficult to know to whom he was speaking, because of that eye. "I suggest that my lord Marischal goes on to the ship first. And when His Grace sets foot on the land, the Kirk then greets him. Only then, we others."

However softly put, that was strangely challenging, and had its effect. None gainsaid it, few in Scotland underestimating the power and influence of this man.

Now, among the crewmen handling the gangway, the slight figure of Charles Stewart could be recognised by such as knew him, his long hair blowing in the wind. Close behind came George Villiers, second Duke of Buckingham, more dandified and foppishly dressed than the monarch, two years older, as had been the first duke to Charles the First, favourites both, which was strange considering how different were the two monarchs themselves.

The chanting rose the higher. What would Charles think of this reception? At least it was no armed threat, as it would have been in England, where Cromwell still ruled, distinctly challenging as it was.

The king came down the gangway, eyeing the chanting divines warily, as well he might. How representative of the Scots people at large were they? Probably but little, in fact, however authoritatively they acted. The common folk were not extreme in their attitudes towards either religion or the monarchy, especially here in the north-east.

With a glance at his Campbell chief, Loudoun the Chancellor spoke up. "His Grace cannot be well versed in conditions here, I judge. He will require much instruction! But, I suggest, not at this first meeting!"

"He will *be* instructed!" the Reverend David Dickson declared briefly. He was of similar seniority in the Kirk to Cant and Blair.

What Charles thought of this chanting reception was not to be known. Had he expected cheering on his arrival in his kingdom?

The Earl Marischal strode forward to be the first to greet the monarch, although the clergy leaders, pushing aside lords and prominent folk, surged close behind him.

That gangway, to be sure, presented a handicap to all concerned. Undoubtedly the earl would have been better to wait at the quayside. For the planking was narrow, not accepting three-abreast without cramping. And it was at quite a steep angle. Here was no possibility of getting down on knees in obeisance – not that any of the divines would have done so anyway.

The Marischal did try to bend one knee as he took Charles's outstretched hand between his own two palms in the traditional gesture of fealty. His welcoming speech, however brief, was drowned in the shouting of "Take the Covenant!"

James, jostled out of the way by the leading clergy, could only watch as the king stood staring down beyond the Marischal at the crowding churchmen who advanced to block the gangway.

He looked from those large, limpid and expressive eyes. His twenty years of life had had their strange moments; this probably was the strangest yet.

Overriding the Marischal's speech, and even outdoing the chanting, came Andrew Cant's sonorous and dogmatic voice. "Sire, we greet you, in the name of Almighty God, the Father, the Son and the Holy Spirit! Amen! By God's grace and permission you come to this ancient land where your forefathers have reigned for a thousand years. It is our duty, as representing the Covenanted Kirk, to require of you, before you set foot on its sacred soil, that you take the Covenant."

A hush had descended, as all stared and waited.

"Take . . . ?" Charles wondered, eyeing the demander, then Buckingham, and back again.

"Aye, *take*, Your Grace. Although, you are *not* Your Grace yet! Take the Covenants, the National and the Solemn League, between Almighty God and His Kirk. Accept and swear to it. As we all have done."

The silence was again broken, this by a tittering laugh. "Ha, Charles, by God, here is play-acting! Better than anything we viewed at The Hague, I vow! I . . ."

Lauderdale raised hand and voice behind the Marischal, to halt this unseemly interjection. But the duke was not finished.

"These are but . . . clerks!" he declared, as though in disbelief.

Cant pointed at him. "Silence!" he cried. "We are God's appointed representatives in this land. How dare *you* to speak! We address and inform the king-to-be. For he is not yet crowned!" That was warning indeed. "Your Grace, it is necessary that you take the Covenant, this before you set foot on the soil of this Scotland."

Charles glanced over at both the Marischal and Lauderdale for guidance, neither earl looking happy.

The Marischal found voice. "This is absurd! Intolerable! To speak so to His Grace. Make way, sirs, for His Grace to land."

"No!" That was Blair. "This is the moment of truth. Do we worship the King of Heaven? Or only the would-be King of Scots!"

"We are not worshipping here. We are welcoming King Charles back to his own land and kingdom."

"Only if he takes the Covenant!"

The other divines shouted agreement.

After the shouting, it was again a soft Highland voice that insinuated itself. "Sire, it would be best, wisest, to agree." That was MacCailean Mor, who had managed to get some way up the gangway. "It will aid your royal cause. You *need* the Kirk. Agree the Covenant, Your Grace, and be welcomed to your realm."

"What is it? To what should I agree?"

Cant answered him. "The three main provisions. You swear to denounce and renounce Popery. To maintain the Reformed Religion in its Presbyterian form. And to adhere to it all your days, banning all episcopacy and bishops."

"But . . ." Charles wagged his head. "How can I do that? Bishops there are, always have been. It is against all the—"

"It is necessary," the other interrupted. "Necessary for your coronation, Charles Stewart. Until you are crowned at

180

Scone, you are not the king. And only the Church of this land can give you coronation. The Kirk!" Here was the secret of the divines' power, and of Argyll's and many others' support of them, although James Hope, for one, doubted.

Into the silence then Buckingham tinkled another laugh. "The masque unfolds! Even the man Shakespeare did not rise to such heights of pretence, Charles! It was worth our journey to hear this!"

Frowning, Loudoun spoke. "Sire, accept it. The form of it is none so grievous. Your Grace's one word will suffice. Then all can be done suitably and in order. We all here seek to welcome you to your ancient kingdom. *All*, I say."

James spoke up. "I do advise that you take the Covenant, Sire. James Graham of Montrose, after all, was its first signatory, those years back."

"But reneged." That was Argyll.

Helplessly, the young monarch shrugged. Had he come from the Netherlands to be faced with this? What *was* this Covenant?

"Do you, Charles Stewart, take the Covenant?" Cant demanded. "Swear to uphold and maintain it?"

The king looked at them all, and his glance lingered on James, whom he knew and trusted. And, at James's nod, he drew a deep breath and said the one word, flatly.

"Yes."

Among the murmurs all around, Cant spoke loudest. "Good. That is well. Your Grace has taken the Covenant. Your coronation is now able to proceed, at Scone, and as near forthwith as may be."

James, for one, was thankful that this extraordinary welcome for a monarch to his kingdom could be accepted as over, and Charles could come down the gangway and set foot on his soil.

Among those waiting there was also Lewis, Marquis of Huntly, the Gordon chief, one of whose castles was the nearest to Garmouth, this why that haven had been chosen for the landing. The hold, lofty, eighty-four feet in height, and large, all but palatial, was named Bog of Gight, its surrounding marshland adding to its strength; indeed the marquis was known locally as the Gudeman o' the Bog. Here Charles was to spend the first night before being escorted down to the Murray Lord Balvaird's house of Scone, on the Tay, for the coronation ceremony at the abbey and Moot Hill there. Even this very large castle was crowded that night, and James had to share a room with Lauderdale and Crichton, Viscount Frendraught. But he managed to gain some privacy, for the immensely thick walling of the building was honeycombed with little mural chambers opening off the rooms, and he was able to bed down in one of these.

Next day the lengthy journey began, its first stage some sixty miles south by east to Aberdeen, all through Gordon country, by Elgin and down Speyside through Strathbogie to Inverurie. A large company, especially including many divines as this did, can never ride fast, the pace having to adjust to that of the slowest. Besides, Charles was to see his country and be seen by his people.

Aberdeen's welcome was not exactly led, but declared, by the provost, proudly wearing his gold chain of office but much flustered at meeting his monarch. He was a fish-merchant. He all but dropped the massive keys of the city on their cushion when presenting them, this just outside the South Gate in the ancient walling. His stumbling speech was interrupted by Andrew Cant drawing Charles's attention upwards to the gatehouse parapet, on which skulls and rag-covered bones projected on spikes, one, as the minister pointed out, the right arm, but handless, of "the renegade and miscreant Montrose!"

The divines more or less dismissed the provost and baillies, and took the royal party through the city, to Marischal College, the former cathedral of St Machar, and the Tolbooth, this last having Montrose's hand nailed to the door, and pointed out, with praises to God. Near by, accommodation was provided for the night in a prosperous merchant's house, with all but strict orders to attend at St Nicholas Kirk at an early hour on the morrow, for it was the Sabbath, this before another service at noonday at the Reverend Cargill's St Machar.

Charles was learning who now ruled Scotland, whoever might *reign*.

After all the Sabbatical proceedings, next day they were for Dunnottar Castle, the Earl Marischal's main seat, on its isolated rock soaring from the cliffs just south of Stonehaven, a score of miles. At least here Charles was able to escape from the clergy, who were installed in the town.

Dunnottar was a dramatic hold indeed, all but impregnable and difficult for even cannon to assail, owing to these being unable to have their muzzles raised sufficiently within range. It rose sheer from the waves save for a narrow access bridgeway, this easily made impassable. It was very ancient, even being a fort of Brude, King of the Picts of Alba in the ninth century, and remaining a proud possession of the monarchial line until coming into the hands of their Earls Marischal, hereditary leaders of their armies.

James was much impressed by it all, and well pleased to be able to lodge therein, with the other leaders of the royal party, up among the wheeling, screaming seafowl, these competing with the sullen and continuous clamour of the waves below.

Plans for the coronation were discussed. This was always traditionally held at Scone, near Perth – and Cromwell had an army thereabouts. How to get this away from there? Some diversion? If General Leslie and his Covenanting host were to make a demonstration down into the west of England, to lure the Roundhead strength thither, then the required area could be freed of them.

Leslie to be besought, then, however doubtful about the monarchy.

The reason why Scone had always been considered so important was that here the fresh water of the River Tay, which was deemed to link Highlands and Lowlands, in the very centre of Scotland, overcame the salt water of the estuary, this seen as ever a symbol of fertility. So it was a sacred spot. Here St Columba's disciples had established a cell, which became an abbey, and nearby a small, conical, isolated hill rose, which had been from time immemorial established as the crowning-place for the High Kings of Alba and their successors, the Kings of Scots. The Moot Hill, as this was named, was alleged to have grown ever higher because, at coronations, the nobles and landholders of Scotland, to indicate that the new monarch in theory held *all* the land for his people from God, each had to bring a handful of soil from his properties, spread it on the hilltop where the king sat on the Stone of Destiny, and, placing a foot upon it, swear fealty to his liege-lord, as it were on his own soil. This ceremony was all part of the coronation.

So, with Cromwell's troops satisfactorily won away south-westwards into England by Leslie, Perth and Scone were freed of the enemy meantime, and the ancient ritual could go ahead. A move was made southwards from Dunnottar.

Two days later James was not the only one to go through the gesture of sampling the water off Scone, tasting various reaches until they found it so little salty as to be accepted as fresh. He had never done this before; but nor had he ever attended a coronation. This on the first day of January.

There was a brief religious service in the abbey-church before the crowning ceremony, at which Cant and Blair and others announced God's wrath against papists, recusants, backsliders and others who did not see the Almighty from *their* perspective.

Then all moved out to the Moot Hill, thankful that the weather was such as to make this no ordeal, New Year's Day as it was. Charles was led up by the officers of state and seated on the throne-like chair. It should have been the Lia Fail, of course, the Stone of Destiny, but that was still somewhere in the Hebrides in the care of the MacDonalds, and they and their like were not represented here.

On the hilltop, the Marquis of Argyll ceremoniously placed the crown on the head of the monarch, to the resounding cheers of the multitude. Then a procession of such lords and lairds as had been prepared to be associated with the so-dominant clergy, which was indeed only a minority, climbed, one after another, to go through the soil-depositing ritual and kneel before the king, holding the royal hand and swearing allegiance and leal duty. This, in the circumstances, did not take so long as was normal, because of absentees, and no very large pile of earth resulted, Charles far from complaining.

He was crowned, that was what mattered to him and to his supporters – and undoubtedly to the majority of the Scots people. England was another affair.

*　　*　　*

But Scotland still had to cope with Cromwell. That man decided that Charles should quickly learn that his northern kingdom was still part of the Commonwealth, and this coronation mere play-acting. He chose to avoid Leslie's threat in the west meantime, and marched north.

Leslie, learning of it, hastened back north-east. Choosing to use the land to aid his cause, as Montrose had done, he put the Forth estuary and river between him and the enemy. He stationed his main force at Falkirk, just south of Stirling, where the bogland and minor rivers would be a handicap to the Roundhead cavalry, as Wallace and Bruce had done, and made his headquarters in the famous Tor Wood.

Cromwell sent one of his lieutenant-generals, John Lambert, to seek to get across Forth at South Queensferry, and to assail the Scots army as it were from behind. At Inverkeithing, where he landed his men, he met a Highland wing of Leslie's force, under Sir Hector Maclean of Duart. These also, vastly outnumbered, fought gallantly; and what became a renowned struggle took place which, although eventually a defeat for the Highlanders, became known as "Another for Hector". This was because that chief, fighting in the lead, had no fewer than seven of his near kin slain at his side, and as one after another fell, summoned more with his cry, "Another for Hector!" Eventually he fell also, but these three words became something of a slogan for the Clan Maclean.

But such gallantry could not alter the military situation as a whole, and Cromwell's Ironsides were scarcely impressed. King Charles had decided to join Leslie in his progress southwards into the English west, although James, Lauderdale and Argyll advised against this. Better, they said, to remain in Scotland, where he had the backing of the people at large, as he did not have in England. But the king said that Leslie's efforts must be supported; and he set off westwards with some of his people, leaving the Earl Marischal to command in Scotland.

Leslie, with Charles now, progressed southwards, and got as far as Worcester before, exactly a year after Cromwell's victory at Dunbar, the Lord Protector caught up with him. He was defeated. Scotland's best general was captured and sent off to the Tower of London, Charles himself only escaping miraculously, aided reputedly by a young woman named Jane Lane, who led him and one or two others off the field by devious routes.

So, where was the young king now? None in Scotland, and few undoubtedly in England, knew.

James, like so many another, wondered. What now? Cromwell must presumably seek to capture Charles; and, dominating the land as he did, somebody would almost certainly betray the king. And then, almost as certainly, it would be execution. Would the monarch's youth spare him the fate of his father? That was doubtful indeed. What could be done to save Charles?

Somehow, he must be got out of the country, both countries. That was probably the wisest course. Have him escape to the Continent. He was young – and Cromwell would not live for ever. Then, eventually, return to his kingdoms. Like so many others, James had sworn allegiance and zealous duty to his sovereign. Was there anything he could possibly do to help fulfil that oath of fealty?

Who would know where Charles was now? After the disaster of Worcester, where would he head? Northwards, probably, back to Scotland, which at least was still loyal to him. But until his whereabouts was known, nothing could be done.

James did make an attempt to do more than just wonder. He took to the saddle, and rode south by west, to make enquiries.

It was Dumfries before he obtained the first information, when the provost told him that the king had passed through the town with two young men, one apparently called Ramsay, and had asked how he could get to Penrith.

Penrith? What, or who, was he seeking at Penrith, among the English lakes? It was none so far over the border.

James rode on thither. And at or near Penrith, at the Howard castle of Greystoke, he did get a clue as to the young monarch's aims, for he heard from the squire there that Charles had been asking where he could get a ship, any merchanter, to take him to the Continent. He had hoped to find such at Dumfries, probably not realising that the Solway Firth was too shallow and tidal for ocean-going craft conveniently to reach the town, and had been advised to head for Workington or Whitehaven, where trading vessels did berth, for wool and smoked meat from the hilly country behind.

That was sufficient for James. Charles was heading for Europe, probably The Hague, from whence he had come, wise in the circumstances, undoubtedly.

He, James, could return home.

Cromwell demonstrated his power. After Worcester, leaving one of his best and effective generals, George Monk by name, to hold Scotland secure, he announced from London that there was no longer a kingdom of that name, any more than was England. Both were to be part of his Commonwealth and Protectorate.

Sadly, Scotland was sorely divided, as ever: Covenanters against Episcopalians, Catholic Highlands against Protestant Lowlands, the clans feuding. So Monk had no major difficulty in keeping military control of a sort.

Oddly, although James much deplored the English domination, he had to admit that the firm sway and authority had its benefits and advantages. Cromwell had achieved what no other English ruler had done, over the centuries, even Edward the First.

To symbolise this situation, Monk sent to London the Chair of State which had been used at Scone coronations as throne; the Holy Cross of St Margaret; and all the important public records and documents on which he could lay his hands. But not, to his frustration, the Honours of Scotland, as they were called, the crown, sceptre and sword of state. These were removed in time to that Dunnottar Castle where Charles had hidden previously. Monk duly besieged it, and when starvation threatened the garrison and surrender seemed imminent, they were most cleverly and gallantly removed by two local women, one of whom, Catherine, was the wife of the parish minister, the Reverend James Granger. She managed to gain access to the castle by carrying a message from the besiegers, and pretending that she was very pregnant, thereafter escaped with the Honours, the long sword and sceptre bound together with cloth to look sufficiently like a distaff to deceive the Cromwellian soldiery; and the crown tucked under her clothing to emphasise her pregnancy. They were taken and buried beneath the pulpit of her husband's church of Kinneff, where they remained for long.

Cromwell demonstrated his abilities in affairs of state, as in war. Probably seldom had England been so efficiently governed, however sternly. To a lesser extent Scotland was also, Monk governing there. Petty crime was put down, the Covenanters were controlled, commissioners were sent north to administer justice in the various regions, although the Highlands could only be dealt with in token, the clans, like their land itself, being scarcely controllable even by the Roundheads. James was allowed to instruct these commissioners where Scots law differed from English, and, although no republican, he had to admit that the monarchial regime had governed less effectively, with less command over the nobility. Scotland had to send thirty representatives down to the London parliament, something never before considered – this although the Scottish assembly continued to sit as a convention. Monk settled garrisons in all cities and large towns.

Lauderdale, like James, recognised that, in the circumstances, some co-operation with the Cromwellian regime was advisable, the earl being allowed to chair the council and the convention, more or less acting Chancellor. Indeed he was sometimes being referred to as the new King of Scotland by opposing lords.

James kept in fairly regular communication with Charles, for trade and shipping was but little interfered with. He was able to reassure that the northern kingdom remained in fair order, not really being oppressed, but remained loyal to the crown. He stressed the effectiveness of Lauderdale, assured that although that man was co-operating with the Protectorate he was nowise disloyal to the monarchy, this attitude applying to himself also, as a practical man. He did suggest, however, that in the circumstances, as more or less the monarch's chief and active representative in Scotland, and to encourage him to further efforts in the royal cause, it might well be a wise move to promote Lauderdale to a higher rank and style, as only the monarch could do. Now that Montrose was dead, the Campbell Marquis of Argyll was the highest-ranking noble in the land. Why not make Lauderdale a marquis? Or, even better, a duke? That would place him in an all but unassailable position to promote the monarchial interests. The only other duke, James, Duke of Lennox and Richmond, was all but an Englishman, living in the south, barely known in Scotland.

In due course the king wrote back. He was indeed raising the earl to the status of duke, which would establish him as, in style at least, supreme in the land, after the monarchy. It was to be hoped that worthy results would accrue. And, in the same letter, Charles again asked, did Sir James not desire himself to be raised in rank? Surely he was suitable to be a Lord of Parliament himself?

James modestly declined. If he became a peer he would inevitably be faced with new duties and responsibilities in connection with the House of Lords, and he had a sufficiency here in Scotland.

There came word from England that Oliver Cromwell was a sick man, and this at a significant time, when he was dividing England into eleven military districts, under that number of major-generals. These commanders, independent of parliament, were proposing that the Protector should now ascend the throne as king himself. As a good republican he was said to be refusing anything such, but nevertheless was seeking to train his son Richard to succeed him in the rule of England – and this Richard was no strong leader and commander, as was the father.

Some in both kingdoms prayed for the Lord Protector's death.

James did not. He recognised that in present circumstances, and the asserted weakness of Richard Cromwell, together with the ambitions and competition on the part of those major-generals, a strong hand was necessary on the helm. In Scotland, Lauderdale could provide that; but in England there would be civil war undoubtedly, between the generals themselves, and with the royalists taking the opportunity to rise against the republicans. And that warfare could spread to Scotland.

With Cromwell's health reported as deteriorating, James decided that King Charles should be advised to take advantage of the situation, and to issue a statement and declaration assuring that, if he was restored to the throne, there would be no vengeance and recriminations against the Roundheads and their supporters, with a general pardon. Also that religious freedom should be accepted. And that the heavy taxation imposed by the Protectorate, to pay for the Cromwellian army, should be reduced – this an important offering, for that financial exaction was much resented by the nobility and common folk alike. It seemed to James that, to convince Charles of all this, it would be best if he himself went to Breda, in the Netherlands, where the king was residing, rather than merely writing letters.

Before he sailed, he had a word with General George Monk, whom he esteemed as a worthy man as well as an able commander. He found him much disapproving of the squabbling major-generals in England, and far from admiring Richard Cromwell. He was, therefore, concerned as to the future in the south. In Scotland, having Lauderdale's and James's co-operation, the situation was under control.

James had learned that Monk had indeed fought for King Charles the First during the English civil war, had been captured at the Battle of Nantwich, and imprisoned in the Tower of London for two years. But he had been released by the Parliamentarians, who respected his military abilities, and sent to Ireland to put down the rebellion there. He had come to terms with the Irish, and was censured therefor by Cromwell. But recognising that Monk could be a very useful lieutenant, the Protector had him released and sent to Scotland to prevent any pro-Charles rising there. Now, in the situation that was developing, James urged him to support the monarchy, as he had done in the past, pointing out that if Cromwell died, as seemed likely, then the weak Richard would make no suitable successor in government, and that both kingdoms would be much better with a monarch who was committed to a moderate and conciliatory reign.

Monk saw the point of this, and, while not committing himself actively to support the king, agreed that James should go to this Breda and seek to persuade Charles to state assuredly and convincingly that, if restored to the throne, he would do all in his power to bring all sides and factions together in peace, by moderate, reconciling and pacific central government. Lauderdale somewhat doubtfully supported this course. James felt that he now had a worthy and valuable mission to perform. He recognised that in this, he, one man, would hopefully make a major impact, on the United Kingdom, on the monarchy and throne, on peace and harmony between the nations – not only Scotland and England but the Netherlands also, for Van Tromp, the Dutch admiral, had already made a spectacular display of his power at sea. Monk and Lauderdale were acceding, but that was all. The onus was upon himself, a mere lawyer. Could he carry the weight of it?

He must try to do so.

Cromwell was reported to be at death's door.

Breda lay in the Netherlands, a dozen miles from the nearest salt water, this at the confluence of the Rivers Mark and Aa.

It took some time to find a merchant ship to take James from Leith to Rotterdam, where, after some more delay, he was able to board a local craft with a cargo of wool, this little more than a large barge, to convey him to the Grevelingen estuary, a subsidiary of the larger Easter Schelde, which got him as near to his destination as was possible by water. There, where the great River Maas joined the estuary, he was able to hire a horse to take him the extra dozen miles due south. Just why King Charles was living there meantime was unclear to James. Perhaps he had some family links with the Duke of Brabant, in whose duchy the small town was located.

He found Breda to be not large but it had a cathedral with one of the highest steeples he had ever seen, factories for linen and carpeting, leather-works and rope-spinning. Also a castle. James spoke no Dutch but he had fair French and managed to make himself understood. At an inn near the castle he enquired whether it was known if the King of England and Scotland was indeed living here, to be told to ask at the castle of Duke Henry of Brabant.

Thither he repaired, and at the gatehouse was told that the duke and his guests were out hunting in the nearby Forest of Soignes. So he stabled his horse at this inn, and waited.

He had consumed a hearty Dutch meal when he heard shouting from the street, and went out and saw quite a cavalcade of huntsmen riding, to great halloo, leading pack-horses laden with dead deer and even a couple of wild boars. And among them was Charles Stewart. James waved, but was not identified amid the townsfolk.

Later, after allowing time for the huntsmen to have had *their* meal, he presented himself again at the castle, declaring that he was a Scottish official of King Charles, to see the monarch. This gained him admission.

He was taken before Duke Henry, a man of middle years, who asked him his business. He said that he had come all the way from Scotland to see the King's Grace, to whom he had been sending letters.

Led to a withdrawing-room, this off the handsome hall where servants were clearing the tables after dinner, James was greeted by laughter. He found Charles in the company of two young women, very much so, for one of them was sitting on his knee and the other pulling his long hair.

The king eyed his entry with astonishment, pointing a finger of his free hand at him.

"Hope!" he exclaimed. "James Hope, by all that is wonderful! My Scottish friend. Here is a surprise! Here, in the Low Countries!"

"Yes, Sire. Come seeking Your Grace."

"You have come a long way, then. What brings you here?"

"You do, Sire. I come, following my letters to you. And in your royal cause."

"So! My royal cause, I fear, is in a sorry state! Or I would not be here."

"It must be bettered, Your Grace. Which is my errand."

The two young women were eyeing James interestedly, the seated one rising.

"These are the Ladies Margrete and Christine, daughters of the Duke Henry. This is my lawyer, from Scotland."

James bowed again. "Your Grace is in good company!"

It was some time, in the circumstances, before he could speak with the king alone; and even then, Charles was in no mood for discussing grave national affairs. But James persisted. He declared that it was vital, not only for the king but for the welfare of his two realms, that the royal authority should be re-established, and that an announcement should be made declaring the king's attitude in the present situation, and his concern and love for his leal people. Cromwell was very ill, indeed could even be dead by now; and his son Richard useless for the nation's governance. If Charles was to regain his throne, as was infinitely to be desired, and by the great majority of his subjects, he should issue a statement assuring that if he was restored there would be no vengeance and recriminations against the Roundheads and those who had supported them; that in fact there should be a general pardon and amnesty for all; that religious freedom was to be accepted; and, highly important, that the heavy taxation imposed by the so-called Protectorate to pay for Cromwell's armies should be reduced.

James was all but urgent about this. The people were in a state of anxiety, upset and confusion. They must be re-assured that the traditional royal authority, restored, would be to their great advantage. A proclamation to that effect to be issued forthwith.

Charles accepted that. Would James make up such statement and proclamation?

Neither realised that this document was going to go down in history as the Declaration of Breda, and represent a milestone in the story of two nations.

James eventually got back to Scotland to learn that Oliver Cromwell was dead.

So what now? All the more urgency for an issuing of the declaration, and Charles's return to his kingdoms, for even the confirmed Roundheads nowise saw Richard Cromwell as an effective leader.

But Charles appeared to be in no hurry to reascend his throne. This Breda seemed to suit him very well. Perhaps it was the young ladies' company? He was obviously that way inclined.

James wrote advising his speedy return, and with Lauderdale's backing. Come to Scotland if he was concerned about his possible reception in London. Oddly this urging was reinforced by, of all people, the Cromwellian commander in the north, George Monk. He had no use for Richard, and deplored the squabbling of the eleven generals. He had decided to throw in his lot with the king. After all, he had served Charles's father loyally. And if he did make this change, many another would undoubtedly do so also. In his letter to the monarch, James recommended that he should tie Monk firmly to his cause. Give him a title, even a dukedom. He could be very useful, a most capable soldier.

And that Charles did, although he himself still remained in the Netherlands. He there and then created George Monk Duke of Albemarle, a squiredom that he had inherited, and besought him to put all Scotland firmly under royal control.

HISTORICAL NOTE

The keen historian may consider that some liberties have been taken on dates and occurrences in this story. But they, more than anyone, will know that the history books can differ widely in their accounts of events and, when telling a story, such as this is, the facts as reported variously must be woven in with as much accuracy as is consistent with a believable tale. The author hopes he will be forgiven.

With the publication of this story we have come to the end of the amazing output of books written by Nigel Tranter, my father. This last was written in his ninetieth year, and his first book, an authoritative work on Scottish fortified houses, was published in 1935. The last eight novels were all finished at the time of his death, as he always kept ahead in his writing, and they have been published posthumously by Hodder & Stoughton, his publishers for many years. I would like to thank them and their editors and assistants. I am proud to have seen the production of all these books go ahead as they complete a long life's work by my father.

Frances May Baker

Nigel Tranter

Marie and Mary

The turbulent sixteenth century is the background for the story of Scotland's most fascinating queens.

Marie de Guise ruled Scotland alone after the death of her husband James V. She foiled Henry Tudor of England's plans to marry her baby daughter to his son Edward and unite the two thrones under English rule by sending Mary to France. And she kept the peace between Protestants and Catholics while John Knox was becoming a fiery power in the land.

Beautiful, lively and clever, Mary Queen of Scots was welcomed back to the country of her birth after her mother died. But her troubles mounted with her disastrous marriages to Lord Darnley and to Lord Bothwell after Darnley's murder. In spite of numerous plots against her, and even after her little son James was crowned king while she still reigned, she always believed that Elizabeth of England would help her.

Trustingly, she set off for England – and her tragic fate.

HODDER

Nigel Tranter

Right Royal Friend

When James the Sixth, His Grace of Scotland, also becomes His Majesty of England, far-reaching changes take place in two realms.

David Murray, the young son of Sir Andrew, a Perthshire laird, has no aspirations to greatness. Then a chance encounter with King James the Sixth leads to him becoming Cup Bearer and Master of the Horse to his young liege. Together with James's foster brother John Erskine, Master of Mar, the three men enter a new era of political intrigue and dynastic manoeuvring.

When David meets and falls in love with Elizabeth Beaton he hopes that he can distance himself from court events and lead a quiet family life in his beloved Perthshire hills. But the demands of a right royal friend lead him straight back into the thick of one of the most notable periods of Scots and English history.

HODDER